KT-244-106

APPOINTMENT WITH VENUS

By the same Author

SEE HOW THEY RUN
SILK PURSE
JILL FELL DOWN
GENTLEWOMEN AIM TO PLEASE
AT DUSK ALL CATS ARE GREY
SOLDIER FROM THE WARS RETURNING
ODETTE

APPOINTMENT WITH VENUS

JERRARD
TICKELL

THE REPRINT SOCIETY LONDON

FIRST PUBLISHED 1951
THIS EDITION PUBLISHED BY THE REPRINT SOCIETY LTD.
BY ARRANGEMENT WITH MESSRS. HODDER AND STOUGHTON LTD.
1953

The characters in this book are entirely imaginary and bear no relation to any living person

PRINTED IN GREAT BRITAIN BY
FERNDALE BOOK COMPANY LIMITED
WORCESTER AND FERNDALE

FOR

DIANA

CONTENTS

CONTENTS

Royal Message to the Channel Islands.

BUCKINGHAM PALACE,
July 9th, 1940.

To the Bailiffs of Jersey and Guernsey.

For strategic reasons, it has been found necessary to withdraw the armed forces from the Channel Islands.

I deeply regret this necessity, and I wish to assure My people in the Islands that in taking this decision, My Government have not been unmindful of their position. It is in their interest that this step should be taken in present circumstances.

The long association of the Islands with the Crown and the loyal service the people of the Islands have rendered to My Ancestors and Myself are guarantees that the link between us will remain unbroken, and I know that My people in the Islands will look forward with the same confidence as I do to the day when the resolute fortitude with which we face our present difficulties will reap the reward of Victory.

GEORGE R.I.

CHAPTER ONE

"MY ORDERS ARE . . ."

At about ten o'clock on the morning of July 10th, 1940, a small motor-boat set out from St. Peter Port in Guernsey for the little island of Armorel. In the bows stood Hans Weiss, captain in the Xth Regiment of Panzer Grenadiers, looking eagerly across the dancing sea towards the distant whale-backed blur on the horizon that was to be his first independent command and his home. He was a man of forty-five, a shrewd, slow-speaking, one-time cattle breeder from Westphalia, and he was well content with his appointment as Commandant of this remote island, for ahead of him lay rest from the thunderstorm of war. There was a light wind and the sea was up. Cormorants stood on the rocks off Herm and once, to his delight, a puffin crossed his bows, skimming the waves at sea level. Captain Weiss smiled with satisfaction and took a deep breath of the morning air.

The blue blur of Armorel hardened and began to assume a definite shape. Weiss took up his field-glasses. After a while, he beckoned his sergeant. Feld-Webel Kurt Vogel clambered forward and wiped the spray from his face.

"*Herr Hauptmann?*"

"We shall be alongside in about a quarter of an hour. You know your orders."

"Yes, *Herr Hauptmann.*" He repeated with parrot-like cynicism a phrase he had learned by heart. "It is the wish of the Führer to respect those whom he has conquered."

"Correct, Sergeant Vogel. These people, these islanders, will be suspicious of us. It is our duty to win them over to our way of life, not by this,"—he laid his hand on the holster of his ten-shot Lueger automatic—"but by patience and by example. These people are not Polish cattle from the ghettos of Warsaw. They have been subjects of the English Crown for centuries; they have a way of life of their own and our task may not be easy. Only time will show."

"I understand, *Herr Hauptmann.*"

The motor-boat came under the lee of the island, turned into the seaweeded entrance of *Havre des Mouettes.* The chugging of the engine died away and the only sound was the soft slapping of the waves on the vessel's sides as she was carried towards the slippery stone steps that led to the quay. The pilot made fast and Captain Weiss stepped ashore, followed by Sergeant Vogel. At the top of the steps, a small group of men waited in silence. Weiss looked from face to face. From each of them he read the same message. It was a message of anxiety and un-understanding. He saluted and said in excellent English:

"Which of you is the Suzerain of Armorel?"

From the group one man stepped forward. He was

an old man with a lined, deeply sunburned face. Unlike the others who wore fishermen's jerseys and cloth caps, he was in a black suit and a bowler hat of ancient shape and lineage. His clumsy black boots were highly polished and dangling from his watch-chain was the image of Queen Victoria. So incongruous was his appearance on this shining morning that Captain Weiss had difficulty in suppressing a smile. The old man said in a voice of great dignity and grief:

"I am the Provost of Armorel. In the absence of our Suzerain it is I who am responsible."

"Then it is to you I speak. The island will be taken over at once and occupied by the armed forces of the Reich. It is my duty to hand you the orders of the German Commandant at Guernsey and these orders will apply to Armorel. Here are the main provisions."

He took a typewritten sheet from his pocket and read aloud:

"All islanders must remain indoors between eleven at night and six in the morning. No boat or vessel may leave any harbour or any other place. No one is allowed to go near the sea or down to the bays. All firearms must be surrendered immediately. All spirits must be locked up and no alcohol may be either supplied or consumed. . . ."

One of the islanders shifted his feet. Captain Weiss looked at him with a swift, calculating glance. He was a red-faced man, his skin lined as was that of his companions. He scowled and licked his lips furtively. By no movement, by no flicker of the eyelids did Weiss let it be seen that in this man he had instantly pin-pointed a possible ally. Here was the contemptible raw material from which might be forged a fifth column. In this poor drunkard's gullet might readily be the seed of corruption—for the Führer scorned no weapon. The domination of Armorel was no military problem to be solved by Panzers and bombers. It was a civilian problem to be solved by the recognition, the isolation and the exploitation of the weakness and frailty of one influential islander. Cupidity, gluttony, fear, lust—each of them or all of them were tools in the hands of the victor and in this case Weiss proposed that the corrupt seed should be nourished into flower by liberal applications of the correct . . . liquid. He caught and held the man's red-rimmed eyes before he went on soothingly:

"This does not apply to stocks of alcohol in private houses or cottages. . . ."

The man's face relaxed.

Captain Weiss folded the typewritten sheet with an air of conscious drama. He was suddenly aware of his rank, his uniform and of the Lueger automatic at his belt. His task was more easy than he had imagined it would be, for these people were made of poor stuff. They stood there before him so humbly, so obsequiously, so silently. He said in curt tones:

"It is also my duty to inform you that any disobedience, no matter how trivial, will be strictly and immediately punished. That must be clearly understood."

He scanned the group. There was no reaction, no protest. The sap had long ago been drained from the spines of these islanders. Ribbentrop was right—and the decadence of the Anglo-Saxons in England had even spread to their remote outposts. It was with a thread of scorn in his voice that he added the well-worn formula:

"It is the wish of the Führer to respect those whom he has conquered."

The Provost said deliberately, "Your Führer has not conquered the country with whom we are one."

Weiss looked at him sharply. The hitherto insignicant figure in the black suit and the ludicrous bowler hat had suddenly acquired significance. The Provost's eyes met his in an unblinking stare. Weiss frowned. Just as he had sensed a potential ally in the drunkard, he now sensed a potential enemy in the Provost. An enemy? It was a big word, much too big a word to describe this puny caricature of officialdom, this ridiculous spokesman for three hundred fishermen, this illiterate guardian of a handful of sea-washed fields. Looking at him, Weiss smiled. He said gently:

"That, my friend, is a question of time. I now wish to say that I hope that you, the islanders of Armorel, will do nothing to make the occupation—unpleasant. That is all. Please lead the way to the Abbaye."

The little group, led by the Provost, began slowly to walk up the *Colline des Mouettes*.

CHAPTER TWO

THE ISLAND

FROM the fifth century to the days of Queen Elizabeth, the island of Armorel had been the lonely haunt of monks, seabirds and pirates. Then, to protect her mariners on their unlawful occasions, the English Queen granted the island to one Hugo Fallaize, a stern and terrible man, appointing him Suzerain and ordering that he and his descendants hold Armorel under the English Crown for ever. For nearly four centuries the islanders were born, lived and died in peace.

Geographically remote from the sinister onrush of science and the quickened tempo of living, the island had preserved the Elizabethan framework of law and of custom. The men were not equipped to walk alone or to direct their actions by an arid rationalism and authority was willingly given to the Suzerain and to the bricks of the Abbaye, the lovely house that had faced the winds since 1565. Over the centuries, all those in trouble had made their way to the Suzerain's door and it was rare indeed that a man or a woman of Armorel left uncomforted. The simple business of the island was run by a group of six elected islanders called *la Court*, who met when necessary under the Suzerain to decide such vital matters as where and when a road should be mended, a field fenced or a boat caulked. The system, indefensible in these enlightened days, resulted in the health and contentment of every man, woman and child on the island, and the Provost had little to do, except to play the harmonium in the church and distribute the Suzerain's bounty.

In the spring of 1938 a grievous blow fell on Armorel. The Suzerain, careless of the weather, was drowned in a sudden squall that blew up from the north-east as he beat back alone from a visit to a sick lighthouseman on the isolated *Rocher des Chèvres*. Two days later, his beloved body was washed ashore off the *Macquereau* to be borne on a farm-cart to the cemetery where so many men and women of his name lay side by side.

Le Roi est mort! Vive le Roi.

His son Luke, young in years but old in his knowledge and understanding of the island and its people, heard the tolling of the church bell surge into a carillon of welcome to the new Suzerain of Armorel, and he squared his shoulders to the task. He showed himself to be a worthy son of his father and the old feudal life of the island reassumed its tranquil pattern, oblivious of the storm that was mounting far from its peaceful shores. There were herring and mackerel in the tides, there were shellfish in the salt pools; the fields of Armorel had to be ploughed, sown and reaped, the cattle had to be milked, the calves led out to the sheltered pastures. Why concern oneself with the folly of other men when the days were strenuous and the nights were for sleep?

A drum beat in Europe.

On the day that war was declared, the Provost of Armorel was summoned to the Abbaye. A special meeting of *la Court* should be called immediately. Standing before his bewildered subjects and friends, Luke Fallaize handed over the island, and the guardianship of all those who lived on the island, into the hands of the Provost.

Armorel should be his care until such time as the guns of the Royal Horse Artillery fired a salute in honour of the victorious English King.

Let us pray.

Within an hour, this young mediæval ruler and his sister sailed out of *Havre des Mouettes* on their way to the battle.

Once again, in little more than twelve months, the traditional organic group had crumbled and the islanders looked at each other with dismay. But the cows were heavy in milk and winter was on its way. There was work in plenty against the bitter months that lay ahead, for the island could no longer rely on sea-borne sustenance. With the advent of war, a new terror had slid into the depths of the sea.

As winter became spring, the wind lifted the salt spray to feed the fields of Armorel. All of a sudden, there were primroses where, an hour before, there seemed only to have been clusters of leaves and the calling of the cuckoo made the island girls look at the men with sidelong glances. The young boys ran to the cliffs and climbed dangerously to the nests, while the gulls screamed at the pillage, their spread wings etched momentarily against the blown backcloth of the March sky. The winds died down and the sap rose. Soon the war would be over and the young Suzerain and his sister would surely come back to their home. But the drive to the Abbaye grew more desolate with weeds, no smoke rose from its ancient chimneys and cobwebs, their filaments sagging with dew, hung from the corners of the shuttered windows.

The summer was long and still. Fearful whispers of attack, retreat and defeat came to the awed ears of the islanders and a new word was muttered in their anxious conversations. The word was "Dunkirk".

On the first day of July, a squadron of German bombers flew low over the fields of Armorel, the sun glinting on their scornful wings. They wheeled to menace the island with their thunder.

Ten days passed, days of rumour, doubt and fear—and, on the tenth day, the Provost put on his black suit and his ridiculous bowler hat and his clumsy, polished boots. In silence he led the members of *la Court* to the harbour and waited for the motor-boat that would bring his Suzerain's triumphant enemies to the ancient steps of the Quai. As the vessel's bows rounded the sea-weeded breakwater, he spoke for the first time. He gave his orders to the island of Armorel in a single word: "Patience."

At the gate to the Abbaye drive, the Provost stopped. He said to Captain Weiss, who was slightly out of breath after the steep incline of the hill:

"May I dismiss the members of the Court?"

"Yes. It is better that I first discuss matters with you alone."

"As you wish." He turned to the silent group of islanders and spoke in the rapid patois of Armorel:

"Return to your homes. There is nothing for you to do—yet. I will talk with this officer and we will all meet in my house this evening at six o'clock. In the meantime, be silent and be patient. Now go."

Without a word, the group dispersed. The gate swung backwards on its rusted hinge.

Walking up the neglected drive in single file, the Provost leading, the procession of three reached the vast oak door of the house. From his pocket the Provost took a huge key and fitted it into the lock. The hall, after the bright sunshine, was a tunnel of darkness. The Provost stepped inside. Weiss glanced at his sergeant with raised eyebrows. He had expected the Provost to stand to one side so that he, the Commandant of Armorel, should be the first to enter the house. He shrugged slightly. Time would change all this—and it might well be necessary to give this gentleman in the bowler hat a lesson in manners. Standing in the gloomy hall, he said curtly:

"You will please show us over the house."

"Very well."

They went over the silent house from cellar to garret. Everywhere the dust lay thick and ghostly sheets draped the furniture. At an oak door leading to a room off the hall, the Provost stopped. He said:

"That is all."

"You have not shown us this room."

"This is the Council Chamber of Armorel. The Suzerain would not wish you to enter it."

Captain Weiss said sharply: "Open the door at once."

"Very well."

The Provost solemnly took off his bowler hat, unlocked the door and stepped into the Council Chamber. He opened the shutters and sunshine streamed into the panelled room. Captain Weiss looked around him with a gasp of astonishment. A long polished oak table shone like glass in the sun's beam and, wonder upon wonder, a silver bowl of fresh dark red roses was mirrored in the shining surface. There were three chairs on either side of the table and, at its head, an elaborately carved oak chair bearing the arms of the island. For a full minute Captain Weiss looked around him, taking in every spotless detail. He said, speaking very softly:

"How comes it, my friend, that in a silent and neglected house, one room alone is prepared for visitors?"

"This is the Council Chamber of Armorel. It is not prepared for visitors. It is prepared for the return of the Suzerain."

There was a long silence. This, Captain Weiss knew with clarity, was the moment of crisis. He was Hauptmann Hans Weiss of the Panzer Grenadiers, Commandant of Armorel, Lord of the Island. He wore the uniform and he carried the weapons of the conqueror.

There was every reason why he should take two, three steps and lower himself into that carved seat of ancient authority, that Royal Throne in miniature. By doing so, by the simple, significant act of sitting down, he could show this black-coated pigmy for once and for all who were the victors and who the vanquished. As a German officer, it was his clear duty so to do. He looked at the Provost, standing humbly before him. He saw the downcast eyes and the red weal in the skin of his forehead made by the unaccustomed hat band. He braced his muscles to take those three utterly decisive steps across the polished floor. The Provost looked up, and the two men gazed at each other steadily. Captain Weiss drew a deep breath. What shameful instinct of gentleness rooted him to where he stood? Captain Weiss didn't know. He only knew suddenly and with certainty that reason was wrong and that instinct was abundantly right. He said in a harsh voice that he recognized with difficulty as his own:

"Sergeant Vogel."

"*Herr Hauptmann.*"

"Take the dust sheets off the table in the dining-room. It will be my office and my orderly room. This Council Chamber is to remain undisturbed."

"*Zum Befehl, Herr Hauptmann.*"

Sergeant Vogel's footsteps made a great clatter in the silent house. The Provost said in a quiet voice:

"I think . . . I think that *Monsieur le Commandant* has made a wise decision."

"I do not seek your approval," he said in frigid tones.

"I demand your obedience. I will summon you in ten minutes and give you my further orders."

"Very well, *Monsieur le Commandant*."

Captain Weiss looked round him once more. It was a beautiful room and he would gladly bury his face in that silver bowl of roses. He strode abruptly into the dark hall. The Provost followed him, carefully locking the door of the Council Chamber behind him.

It was strange for the Provost to stand in the dark and dusty hall waiting for the moment when it would please the German officer to call him. Although it was not yet midday, the Provost felt very tired and it seemed that strength, both physical and mental, had been drained out of him. He yawned prodigiously. He was aware that a battle had been fought and won. But he knew that it was only the first of a series of battles that would have to be fought over the months, possibly over the years to come, and he was dismayed by the weight of time on his shoulders. He could hear the German officer talking gruffly to his sergeant and the sound of furniture being moved. He walked to the hall door, opened it and stood blinking at the weedy drive and the sunlit pastures below. All Armorel seemed to be utterly deserted. How soon would those quiet roads resound to the tramp of marching men, breaking the old tranquillity of the island noon? If only, if only he were a younger man. . . .

"The *Herr Kommandant* will see you now."

"Very well."

The Provost followed Sergeant Vogel into the dining-room. Captain Weiss sat at the dusty table. He had taken off his peaked cap and for the first time the Provost had time to see the man as he was. It was a good face, the face of an honest man. His eyes were of an almost metallic blue and he looked lean and hard and fit. There were tiny lines at the corners of his eyes and the mouth was set into what the Provost instinctively knew to be a deliberate, unaccustomed severity. Captain Weiss said curtly:

"Please sit down."

The Provost carefully placed his bowler hat on the table and sat down.

"What is your name?"

"I am the Provost of Armorel."

"You prefer to be addressed by your office and not by your name?"

"Yes. It is the custom of the island."

"I will be frank with you, *Monsieur le Provost.* We seek your goodwill and your co-operation. We will do what is within our power and our dignity to acquire both. But there is a point beyond which we will not go. We will respect your customs, but we will not tolerate obstinacy or obstruction. What is your name?"

"My name is Jacques le Cheminant, Provost of Armorel."

"Thank you. I propose, for the time being, to retain you in your office. You have heard our general orders. Here is a typewritten copy which you will post up on the door of the Abbaye for all to see. I now come to a few particular points. Please give me your attention. All firearms and all wireless sets must be surrendered at once. They will be brought to the Abbaye this afternoon and handed to Sergeant Vogel, who will acknowledge their receipt in writing. The telephone exchange and the lighthouse will be vacated immediately and will be taken over by technical units of the German Army who are arriving in Armorel this afternoon. In the meantime, no islander, other than you, *Monsieur le Provost*, may use the telephone for any purpose whatsoever. I noticed that when you dismissed your companions this morning you spoke to them in the patois of the island. The occupying troops have been handpicked for their knowledge of English and the speaking of patois is banned absolutely."

The Provost raised one hand, let it fall helplessly. He said, frowning:

"I do not wish to make difficulties, but *Monsieur le Commandant* will understand that we have spoken our own language over the centuries and it comes readily to our tongues. It will not be loved if we are commanded to forget what we absorbed with our mother's milk."

"There are many things that the islanders will have to learn to forget," said Captain Weiss drily. "Let this be the first lesson. I forbid the speaking of patois."

Even as he spoke, he knew with bitterness that it was criminally foolish to issue a command that was incapable of enforcement. In their cottages and their fields, by their firesides and their fuchsias, the islanders would continue to talk patois. As a result of this order, they would talk it secretly and with furtive glances. In a moment of resentment he had wilfully created a bond of shared subversiveness amongst those he wished to unify in obedience. He hesitated. No. It was too late to retract. He said harshly, despising himself:

"Any islander overheard speaking patois will be severely punished."

"Very well, *Monsieur le Commandant.* I will transmit your order to my friends of the Court, who will make it known. I can do no more than that."

"There are the rest of my orders. The blackout will be strictly observed. As more German troops arrive, you will make arrangements to house them. I expect a total garrison of about fifty men and three more officers. As regards food, the garrison will be sustained from Germany by way of Guernsey. You will prepare for me a census of the island, as well as a census of stock on the island. I have here a map of Armorel. As soon as time permits, you will escort me or my officers over every inch of every field. Now, I would like you to give me a brief description of the island's customs and system of government."

The Provost considered the dusty floor for some moments. When he spoke it was with long, inarticulate pauses between his words.

"*Monsieur le Commandant*, you ask me to explain things which are known to all of us and honoured by all of us, but there are things which are very hard to make clear to a stranger. As to our customs, you will observe them yourself as time passes"—he sighed—"and they will become known to you. Our system of government may seem simple to you, but its strength lies in the looseness of its fabric."

Captain Weiss raised his eyebrows. These were strange words in the mouth of this island Socrates, this unarmed, elected policeman of farmers and fishermen. He sat back and said genially:

"Proceed, my friend. I confess to you that I did not expect a dissertation on political philosophy but, believe me, I am all attention."

The Provost blinked and studied his gnarled fingers.

"I do not understand what you say about . . . about political phil . . . phil . . . I do not know the word. I seek only to answer your question. Our Suzerain is the father of the island. It does not matter if he is young like our Suzerain is young, or old like I am. He is still the father of us all. After the Suzerain comes the Provost. The Provost is nominated by the Suzerain and freely chosen by the islanders. Then there is——"

"One moment. If, as you say, the Suzerain is the father and the Führer of you all, how could the island possibly dispute his choice of Provost?"

"He is our father, not our Führer. And the Suzerain would never nominate as Provost one who was unacceptable to the island. He is first of all one of us and he knows our ways. That is simple. The members of the Court come to be chosen and I don't know how. One day a man is a fisherman, the next day he is still a fisherman but also a member of the Court, and he wears the authority of the Court like his clothes. One day, for no reason at all, the herring are in the tides. It is like that."

Captain Weiss leaned forward intently.

"This Suzerain of yours, where is he?"

"I don't know, *Monsieur le Commandant*. He went away the day that war was declared, he and his sister."

"You mean the pair *ran* away, leaving you, an old man, to bear responsibilities which should be his."

"They did not run away, monsieur. They went away to join the forces of His Majesty, to fight for the great union of which we in Armorel are proud to be a tiny part."

"So."

Captain Weiss sat back. A feather of anxiety touched his heart. He saw difficulty ahead, difficulty and danger. Crossing from Guernsey, the morning had been so fresh and beautiful and the island had seemed in prospect to be a haven from the sounds, the dirt and the cruelty of war. Now he sensed a new conflict, a conflict that would be the more bitter because it would be fought in silence far from the turmoil and the triumph of the battlefield. But the battle went to the strong, and at this moment all Europe lay in chains at the feet of his Führer. Across a contemptible puddle of sea, the German army stood flushed with victory and terrible with weapons. It was a reassuring vision in this silent house and it brought a strong surge of confidence to his mind and muscles.

"Tell me, when this Suzerain of yours . . . left, did

he only take his sister, or did he take the whole of his family with him?"

A shadow crossed the old man's face. He said slowly:

"One member of the Suzerain's family remains in Armorel. Only one."

"Oh. Who is this?"

"He is the cousin of our Suzerain. He is Mr. Lionel Fallaize."

"Ah. You will be good enough to present my compliments to this dilatory princeling and instruct him to call on me here at three o'clock this afternoon."

The Provost said in obvious distress, "I would like to say that Mr. Lionel, although of his family, is not in any way like our Suzerain. I . . . I would not like *Monsieur le Commandant* to make a mistake and judge those who are absent by one who chose to remain."

Captain Weiss stood up and put on his peaked cap. He smiled again.

"What you tell me interests me more and more. I feel sure that your Mr. Lionel and I will find much in common. He is to present himself to me—here—at three o'clock."

"Monsieur, he may not wish to come."

"In that case, I will send Sergeant Vogel to fetch him. My sergeant is not as I am, *Monsieur le Provost.* He will take his revolver with him. Now show me the way to the wine cellars and tell me where I can find a corkscrew." He paused and said soothingly, "Pray do not distress yourself concerning your master's cellar. Every drop I drink will be replaced. I must remind you that the bounty of France and of her vineyards is at our disposal."

In the silent hall Captain Weiss stopped by the ancient grandfather clock and opened its walnut case. Slowly he wound up the two weights, moved the hands to ten to one, set the pendulum swinging. The steady tick-tock, tick-tock was a pleasant sound for him to hear. He put a genial hand on the Provost's shoulder.

"You see. Life starts once more in the Abbaye. Now I hope you will join me in a glass of your master's wine."

"I think that *Monsieur le Commandant* has much to learn about the people of Armorel," said the Provost sadly.

CHAPTER THREE

PORTRAIT OF THE ARTIST

LIONEL FALLAIZE stood at his easel overlooking the *Pointe de Joie* in Armorel and painted what was in his vision. Below him the sea was a web of grey silk in the July haze and over the far blue blur of Sark a wisp of white cloud hung motionless. Lionel saw neither the sea nor the land. He saw Sark as the frantic blue eye of a mad woman and the cloud as her white eyebrow. He had yet to decide what monstrous creatures lurked beneath the grey of her skin.

He was a man of about twenty-eight, tall, lean and cadaverous. The movements of his hands were restless and he painted in sudden spurts, almost flinging his oils on to the white canvas, stopping work abruptly to stare for minutes on end into the yellow hub of the sun. He wore paint-stained flannel trousers, buckskin shoes, a cream silk shirt and a Wykehamist tie. During one of his long, abstracted pauses he heard footsteps on the road and swung round with a scowl, resentful of interruption. He saw a strange, hard-faced man in a grey-green uniform and a forage cap. As the man approached him, Lionel saw with incredulity that he carried a long-barrelled revolver in his hand and that his eyes were like slate.

"You are Mr. Lionel Fallaize?"

"Yes. I am he. You must be a German soldier. Bless me! How odd that you should be here." He glanced quickly at his wrist-watch and ran his fingers through his hair. He said, "Oh Lord."

"The Provost instructed you to report to the Commandant of Armorel at three o'clock."

"Yes. The Provost did mention something about it, but I'm afraid that I became absorbed in what I was doing and I had no idea of the time."

"It is now more than four o'clock."

"Yes, I'm afraid it is." He looked at Sergeant Vogel's revolver and said with a faint petulance, "Do put that idiotic thing away. It might be loaded."

"It is loaded."

"Well, then, put it away like a good fellow. If it's loaded, it might go off."

"You will come with me to the Commandant at once."

"Look here," said Lionel, "I take it that your Commandant will be staying here—for a few days at least. I don't know his plans. The point is that I have waited for weeks for that quality of light over Sark." He waved his brush towards the veiled sun. "Its texture is like tweed. Would you ask your Commandant if I may call on him in about an hour and a half?"

Sergeant Vogel's face was suddenly suffused. He half-shouted in the stillness of the afternoon: "You are insolent. In Poland you would be flogged and then shot."

Lionel blinked. "Insolent—no. Absent-minded—

yes." He went on, screwing his eyes up with the queerly pedantic air of a lecturer. "And let me tell you that murder, whether in Poland, Patagonia or anywhere else, is no solution to any problem. Assassination is the outcome of mental and intellectual bankruptcy and all it does is to create a host of new problems. To silence one tongue by violence sets a thousand tongues wagging. The toxin generates the anti-toxin and——"

Sergeant Vogel had changed his grip from the butt of his revolver to the barrel. He suddenly swung his arm up and hit Lionel a blow across the mouth. Lionel fell back, knocking over his easel. A gush of blood started to his lip and crawled in a red trickle down his chin. Holding a silk handkerchief to his mouth he scrambled to his feet and faced Sergeant Vogel. He was breathing deeply and his knuckles showed white in his sunburned hands. He said a little unsteadily:

"From the days of Seneca one has heard of *furor teutonicus* as one hears of a disease. My . . . my diagnosis of your condition is complete. Now I would like to meet your Commandant and apologize for my apparent discourtesy."

"*Hier ist Herr Fallaize, Herr Hauptmann.*"

"Thank you, Sergeant. He is not 'Herr' but 'Mr.' Fallaize. That is all. You will wait outside."

"*Zum Befehl, Herr Hauptmann.*"

Sergeant Vogel marched out of the dining-room of the Abbaye. Captain Weiss looked steadily at Lionel Fallaize. He opened his cigarette-case and extended it.

He said politely, "Won't you have a cigarette and sit down, Mr. Fallaize?"

"Thank you. I don't smoke. But I'd like to sit down. I must apologize for being late. I was painting and in Armorel punctuality is not one of our virtues. Time is our servant and not our master. Believe me when I say I did not wish to be deliberately rude."

"I see that . . . you have had a slight accident, Mr. Fallaize."

"Yes. I slipped. It's nothing much. It will heal."

"May I offer you a little brandy?"

"No, thank you. This is nothing."

Captain Weiss contemplated the thread of smoke from his cigarette. He said at last:

"May I ask you a few questions?"

"Certainly."

"While waiting for you, I confess that my curiosity got the better of me and I spent a profitable half-hour amongst the pages of that admirable reference book called *Who's Who*." He opened the book and began to read. "I see that you were born in 1912 and that you are the only son of Major-General Sir Mark Fallaize, K.C.B., D.S.O., M.C., and of Heloise, e.d. of Rear-Admiral Algernon Marlowe, R.N. (Ret.). What does 'e.d.' mean, Mr. Fallaize?"

"Eldest daughter."

"Of course. I see that you were educated at Winchester and St. Jude's College and that you are a B.A. (Oxon). What subject did you study at Oxford, Mr. Fallaize?"

"Byzantine Greek."

"Interesting. . . . You are a painter and essayist and, while still an undergraduate, you founded and edited a monthly magazine called *Chaos* which was banned by the Proctors and publicly burned on Magdalen Bridge by members of your own College Eight. It then says, 'A frequent if involuntary bather in Mercury.' That I do not understand."

"No, I don't suppose you do. 'Mercury' is the name of a goldfish pond in the House—in Christ Church that is—and unpopular people are apt to be chucked in, in their clothes. It's all very childish."

"In Heidelberg, our students slash each other's faces with swords."

"That is even more childish."

"A matter of opinion, Mr. Fallaize. Finally, I see that your recreations are the propaganda and practice of pacifism, and the study of Serbian pottery." He shut the book with a smile. "You appear, on your own showing, to be a somewhat complex character. One would seek you in Chelsea, or in Montparnasse, rather than in this remote island."

"I live here because, as a conscientious pacifist, I refuse to have anything whatsoever to do with this lunatic war. Here, until you came to-day, I was a free man. I could paint the things my fingers wanted to paint, without a lout in uniform, any country's uniform, yours or mine, telling me where I must or must not go."

"But you are the son of a distinguished soldier and the nephew of a British Admiral."

"I do not see why that should alter my views." He half-smiled. "It may even be the cause of them. The fact is that I am neither soldier nor sailor. I am a painter. I am an individual, not an automaton."

"And because you are an individual, you stay here while your country is at war and paint pretty pictures."

"My pictures are not pretty. I hope that they are significant."

"I am no art critic, Mr. Fallaize." He shook his head, frowning. "Your family has a most honourable tradition of service under the British crown. In spite of what you say, I find it difficult, as a German, to believe that you can sincerely think as you claim—and even more difficult to believe that the British Government would permit you to practise what you claim to think. Shall I tell you what is in my mind?"

"Please do."

"I am wondering if you are here for a purpose."

"What purpose?" said Lionel with interest.

"To work in secret for the British Government."

Lionel laughed, and immediately dabbed the corner of his mouth with his handkerchief. He said:

"You must come to tea and see my false beard. Or do you think I signal to the Royal Navy with a paint-brush?"

"It is no subject for laughter, Mr. Fallaize. Remember Norway and Denmark. Remember Holland, Belgium, France. The German armies only attacked from without when the enemy was already rotted from within. It could be that you are here to sustain the islanders and sap the strength of the German garrison."

"You flatter me."

"Not at all. I have a great respect for the British Intelligence Service. The English are slow to learn a new technique but, once learned, they are its masters for ever."

"I have told you that I am neither soldier nor sailor. I now add that I am neither fifth columnist, saboteur nor spy. I live on Armorel for no reason other than to put on to canvas what is in my vision and my mind. I regard war as a form of mass insanity and I refuse absolutely to have anything to do with it. It is as simple as that."

Captain Weiss looked at him shrewdly.

"Shall I tell you what would happen to a 'simple' person—such as you claim to be—in Hitler's Reich? You would be taken to Berlin, to the prison of Alexanderplatz, and there you would be beheaded with an axe. By the new law of Hermann Göring, you would be beheaded looking upwards so that you could see the man who held the axe and the axe descending."

"I would prefer to be the victim of violence"—his fingers strayed involuntarily to his mouth—"than do violence to another."

"Oddly enough, I am inclined to believe you—against my better judgment. You have not yet explained to me how it came about that you cut your lip."

"I slipped, that's all." He shrugged. "It was an accident. I . . . I have only myself to blame."

Captain Weiss said slowly, "I think that you may well be what the English call 'a gentleman', Mr. Fallaize."

Lionel stood up. He said frigidly:

"There is no subject of discussion so trivial as that of social distinctions. In England, such conversations are confined to the servants' hall. Have I your permission to leave?"

A tiny pulse began to beat at Captain Weiss's temple. With an effort he kept his voice easy.

"Of course, Mr. Fallaize. We will meet again, many times. By the way, my name is Weiss, Hans Weiss. In the new conditions I most sincerely hope that you will continue to confine your activity on the island—to painting. I find your company most stimulating and I should be sorry indeed to . . . lose you."

"I have no activity other than painting. I only ask to be left alone. Good-bye, Mr.—or I should say Captain—Weiss."

"*Auf Wiedersehen,* Mr. Fallaize."

Captain Weiss sat on the edge of the dining-room table, swinging his legs in their field boots. He put on his peaked cap and his gloves.

"Sergeant Vogel."

Sergeant Vogel came running from the kitchen, stood stiffly to attention.

"*Zum Befehl, Herr Hauptmann.*"

"Did you strike Mr. Fallaize, Sergeant?"

Sergeant Vogel hesitated. He stammered a little.

"*Herr Hauptmann,* I . . . I . . ."

"So you did strike Mr. Fallaize. Did you strike him with your fist?"

Sergeant Vogel glanced nervously at Captain Weiss. His face was impassive, but Vogel saw the tiny pulse beating steadily at his temple. He twisted his fingers.

"*Herr Hauptmann*, Mr. Fallaize was insolent. I hit him with the butt of my revolver."

"I do not believe that he was insolent, Sergeant. Mr. Fallaize is a man of courtesy." He stood up, softly smiling. "When you hit Mr. Fallaize with the butt of your revolver, did he expect the blow?"

"No, *Herr Hauptmann*."

Suddenly Captain Weiss drove his gloved fist into Sergeant Vogel's mouth. He shouted in a voice of thunder: "And did you expect that blow?"

Sergeant Vogel swallowed a mouthful of blood, gulped and stood rigidly to attention:

"No, *Herr Hauptmann*."

"You are a fool and a dolt. It is fools and bullies like you who make the name of Germany hated in the world. You have given an Englishman the right to talk to me, a German officer, of the servants' hall and I have no answer. That is what you have done. If ever you lift your hand to a living thing on this island again, I will shoot you like a dog. Now get out."

"*Zum Befehl, Herr Hauptmann*."

The Provost's whitewashed cottage and his neat front garden were enclosed by a hedge of veronica and fuchsia. One by one, the members of the Court arrived unobtrusively to lift the polished brass horseshoe knocker and to hang their cloth caps on the antler hatstand in the hall. By five past six, the last of them had come and the Provost, his formal black suit discarded in favour of blue serge and a fisherman's jersey, shut the parlour door.

The six men stood round the parlour table with its fringed plum plush tablecloth and its aspidistra in a gleaming brass pot. The Provost looked from face to face. He said, "*Prions Dieu.*"

Every head bent. The Provost spoke in the French that had been known to the island since the day when Hugo Fallaize, first Suzerain of Armorel, had set foot on Armorel.

"*Notre Père, qui êtes aux Cieux . . .*"

The parlour, with its hermetically sealed windows and its lace curtains, smelt of yellow soap, oil lamps and mice. A fan of pink paper was spread over the empty grate and on the wall hung a fly-spotted oleograph of a terrible shipwreck. It was called "The Loss of the Frigate *Wilhelmina*". A photograph of the Provost's sailor son—drowned in H.M.S. *Hampshire* in 1916—gazed woodenly out of a heart-shaped red plush frame at a printed certificate stating that Jacques le Cheminant was a member of the Royal Ancient Order of Buffaloes. The Provost's voice was full of meaning as he repeated the centuries-old supplication:

"*Oh, Dieu tout-puissant, Roi des rois . . . Sauvez-nous et delivrez nous de la main de nos ennemis. . . .*"

What sin had these men committed that they should be meted out with such terrible and bewildering punishment? With deep reverence, the Provost finished the ancient prayer and gazed for a moment at the ceiling. He went on, hesitating over the unfamiliar words:

"*Notre Seigneur* . . . Thou who knowest all, will understand our distress at this time. We ask Thee to give us patience and fortitude and to protect us and those we love from the malice of our enemies in the hard days that lie ahead." He stopped and clasped his hands.

"*Illumine nos ténèbres, Oh Seigneur; et par ta grande miséricorde garantis-nous de tous les dangers et tous les accidents de cette nuit. . . .*"

There was a low rumble of voices as the Court joined in the final "Amen". The Provost went to the door and opened it and called, "Marie". His wife, who had been waiting for his summons, came into the parlour with a tray on which stood a bottle of rum, seven tiny liqueur glasses and a plate of cake. She wore a white apron over her black satin dress, a heart-shaped locket and button boots. She shook hands with each of the men and left the room without a word. The Provost poured out a minute measure of rum into each glass and the men took the glass thimbles in their enormous hands. There was hardly enough rum in each glass to wet the tips of their tongues, but this was an occasion when the formalities of polite drinking must be observed and they waited awkwardly for their host to give a toast. He raised his glass:

"I drink to the return of our Suzerain.

"To our Suzerain."

The Provost sat down in a hideous Victorian armchair. He spoke in Armorel patois:

"My friends, there is little for me to tell you that you do not know. The speaking of patois is forbidden, but the German officer knows already that that is a foolish order and I do not think that he will enforce it. All firearms and wireless sets are to be surrendered. I have thought deeply about this and I have decided that one wireless set must be kept back. Without knowledge of our mother country and the outside world, we might at last come to believe all that our enemies cared to say to us, and I think that the Germans will tell us many lies. It is also possible that the Germans will search our homes and, because of this, I have hidden my wireless set in a . . . place. I will listen to London at a varying time every day and I will find means of telling one of you the news. Whoever hears it will pass it on to another, and so the island will know the truth. The German officer saw Mr. Lionel this afternoon. I do not know what passed between them, but I am sure that from Mr. Lionel we have nothing to fear. Though the Hand of God is heavy upon him, he is one of us. Baptiste, the cowman, will continue to work the farm of the Abbaye and he will see and tell us of the movements of our enemies." He looked at one man, the red-faced man who had licked his lips that morning in the harbour. He said, lifting one hand in mute apology, "We of the Court are a chain. But the strength of the chain lies in its weakest link. In this difficult moment, I speak to you alone, Jean. I am your old friend. You are a good man, but when your thirst is on you, you could destroy us all. You have just drunk a glass of rum in honour of our Suzerain. I beg of you to let that be the last glass you drink until our Suzerain comes back to us."

Jean shuffled his feet. He said with embarrassment:

"It will be so, *Monsieur le Provost.* I have been foolish in the past. Now it is finished."

"You promise this—before the Court?"

"I promise. In the name of God."

"So be it. I am well content, Jean." He looked around the group. "Is there anything else I can tell you?"

"The German officer—what is he like?"

The Provost frowned. He said at last:

"I think he is a good and an honourable man. In his heart, he will not like the things he may do. Only time will show. We must be patient, patient and watchful. But I believe that he could be our friend."

In the dining-room of the Abbaye, Captain Weiss sat alone. Imperceptibly, the quality of the light had changed and there was a dimness in the corners of the room. He had been sitting at this table for a long time, and now he didn't even hear the slow tick-tock, tick-tock of the clock in the hall. That comforting sound had long ago woven itself into the silence of the house.

He knew with sadness that the fruits of victory were sour in his mouth. No longer did he see himself as Captain Hans Weiss, Panzer Grenadier, Commandant of Armorel, lord of an ancient island. He saw himself, instead, as a solitary, lonely man, isolated forever from those he would wish to make his friends by the eternal and inescapable curse of his German blood.

CHAPTER FOUR

WHITEHALL

ALBERT RADNOR, a clerk in the Ministry of Agriculture and Fisheries, strolled along Whitehall from the Silver Cross where he had been having a nice pint of beer and a sandwich for his lunch. An old man was selling *Evening Standards* by the door of the Ministry, and Albert bought a copy. He made his way along endless corridors to a door marked "Cattle Division" and entered, hanging up his bowler hat. Then, as it was not quite two o'clock, he put his feet up on his desk and settled down to give his somewhat somnolent attention to the European scene.

The date was July 14th, 1940. In France, it had been proclaimed a day of national mourning by old Pétain —and well it might, he thought. Old Hitler had certainly hit the Froggies for six and they had plenty to mourn about. Albert read of invasion barges being ominously marshalled, of German bombers being moved up to within striking distance of the Kentish coast. He yawned and turned to page three. According to old Musso, the Italians were massing for an attack on British Somaliland. Blasted sauce, that's what it was! Just as he had dismissed Joan of Arc, Napoleon, Pétain and all Frenchmen, living or dead, by the word

"Froggies", so did he now dismiss all Italians from Nero to Musso by the word "Wops". Page five yielded the report of a speech made by old Molotov in Moscow. Mr. M. had reaffirmed Soviet neutrality and the peaceful purpose of the non-aggression pact with old Hitler. Unfortunately, he had then gone on to describe the British as "pluto-democratic wolves" and various other things that were a bit off. Albert sighed.

It didn't matter if they were Froggies, Wops or Bolshies. All foreigners were the same. Mind you, some Yanks weren't bad. Old Roosevelt was all right but, by and large, foreigners were *na-poo*. It was a relief to turn to the cricket page and read about something human.

An absorbed quarter of an hour passed. Albert was about to put the paper down and start in on the afternoon's work when a smudged paragraph in the Stop Press caught his eye. He read it lazily. Then he read it again with more attention—and stared, frowning, into the corner of the room. He scratched his head and re-read the message for the third time:

ARMOREL OCCUPIED

It is now claimed (by the Hamburg radio) that the island of Armorel, smallest of the Channel Islands, has been occupied by elements of the German Army.

According to Hamburg, no resistance was offered. Armorel is the last of the Channel Islands to fall.

With deliberation, Albert took his feet off his desk and walked to a filing cabinet. After a moment or two, he found what he sought, a buff-coloured folder marked VENUS DE L'ABBAYE: *Future Progeny Schedule.* He opened the folder and carefully studied a sheet of paper. Then he counted up to nine on his fingers, checking his mysterious calculations on the desk calendar. He frowned again and suddenly appeared to come to a decision of importance. He combed his hair with a pocket comb, straightened his tie and, taking the folder and the *Evening Standard* in his hand, walked out of the room and along the passage to a door marked EXECUTIVE OFFICER. He was blissfully unaware that the deferential tapping of his knuckles on that civilian door was to sound like the beating of a drum in the corridors of the War Office.

Blown by the winds of enthusiasm, the buff-coloured folder flew at unprecedented, breakneck speed along the usual channels. It darted like a swallow from "In" to "Out" trays, skilfully avoiding the awful nets of the "Pending", and flew on. Embellished by a riot of URGENT, IMMEDIATE and FOR ACTION labels, it came breathlessly to rest on the virgin blotter of one Robert Carruthers who not only ranked as a "Principal" in the Ministry, but who was also an amateur breeder of Dairy Shorthorns.

Carruthers' expert eye swiftly sorted the problem. Though he loved his Dairy Shorthorns with a fierce, exclusive love, this was no time to be partisan. The wider challenge was clear. He took the file in his hands and entered the office of his chief, Humphrey Petherton, O.B.E.

With reluctance, Mr. Petherton detached his mind from a question dear to his heart, the potential psychological reaction of artificial insemination on cross-bred chickens, and consented to read the contents of the folder.

At first sight, the matter appeared to be a trivial one and he wondered why it should have been brought to his attention. It was with a touch of acerbity that he took off his spectacles.

"This file, Carruthers, appears to concern a cow, a bovine aristocrat rejoicing in the name of Venus de l'Abbaye. Is one correct?"

Carruthers sensed the displeasure that veined his precision of speech.

"You are correct, sir."

"Then may one ask in what way one is involved in the welfare of this . . . er . . . lactatory goddess?"

"Well, sir, Venus is in calf to a bull called Mars and——"

Mr. Petherton raised a slim hand, enjoining silence.

"I am happy to hear it. If indeed one is to dignify the beasts of the field with the names of gods, I am relieved to know that there can be no question of celestial *mésalliance*. Pray continue."

"Venus is an animal of flawless pedigree. So was Mars."

"You use the present indicative in relation to Venus,

the imperfect (or past) in relation to her . . . er . . . consort. Why? Is the redoubtable Mars no longer with us?"

"No, sir. Immediately after consorting with Venus —'serving' is the technical word—Mars had the misfortune to step on an uncharted landmine. Literally in a flash, the result of ten generations of fine breeding became, as it were, fillet of steak for the hungry inhabitants of Armorel."

Mr. Petherton sighed sentimentally.

"Who was it, Carruthers, who said that death is the perfect end to every love-affair, for then there can be no end? Be that as it may, for your Venus to eat the grass of Armorel must, in itself, be a consolation for her abrupt widowhood. In the tranquillity of that island of honeysuckle, no income-tax and no death duties, she can wear her widow's weeds with composure." He was all at once weary of the subject and said testily, "You are taking an inordinately long time to come to the point. What is it?"

"The point is this, sir. For years we've been trying to get the Mars-Venus strain. At last we've succeeded —and, within her, Venus carries the first of a noble line." He added bitterly, "It may also be the last."

"But why? The animal shall have the most skilled veterinary attention. A bovine gynæcologist will be specially flown to Armorel to assist at this Homeric confinement. No trouble or expense will be spared, no avenue will remain unexplored, no stone left unturned." He chuckled. "Since time began, every father has suffered needless anxiety about the advent of his firstborn. Pull yourself together, my dear fellow. All will be well."

Carruthers blinked rapidly. He had been up for most of the night filling sandbags, he was dog-tired and suddenly impatient of his chief's elephantine humour. When he spoke there was an edge to his voice like that of a rusty razor blade.

"It may interest you to know that the island of Armorel is now occupied by the Germans and any airborne bovine gynæcologist who set out from England would be blown out of the sky by the Luftwaffe."

"Dear me!" said Mr. Petherton petulantly. "Nobody told me about this. Nobody ever tells me anything. . . ."

"Venus and her unborn calf are therefore Hitler's prisoners—unless . . ."

"Unless what, Carruthers?"

There was a long silence. Outside in St. James's Park a barrage balloon ascended slowly to sway, sun-flecked, in the summer sky. Mr. Petherton said incredulously:

"Surely you are not going to suggest, Carruthers, that I should put this file to the Service departments?"

Carruthers thought of his Dairy Shorthorns, his sturdy bull, his young heifers, his full-bellied cows, heavy in milk. They were safe and secure in the unassailable fields of England. He said obstinately:

"I would like your permission, sir, to put it across to the War Office—for action."

CHAPTER FIVE

BLUEPRINT FOR DANGER

THE occupation of Armorel was carried out with unusual discretion. The German soldiers arrived without fuss and marched in silence up the hill to the commandeered hotel which was to be their barracks. One detachment went to the lighthouse, another to the telephone exchange. A sentry was posted at the gate of the hotel drive. He was a young man of about twenty, unarmed and smiling. The children gazed at him wide-eyed from behind the hedges, as he leisurely paced up and down in the sunshine. Soon the boldest of them ventured on to the road to stand and stare. The sentry stopped and felt in his pocket, found an apple. He said, still smiling: "You wish an apple?"

The little boy made no movement. The sentry said:

"You will please catch the apple in your hands."

He threw it. Still the boy remained dumb and immobile. The apple fell at his feet, rolled a few inches, came to rest in a wheel rut. The sentry shrugged and continued his leisurely pacing. Two hours later, when he was relieved, the apple was still untouched, but the boy had been joined by two little girls and a mongrel dog. They watched the formal change-over with interest and without fear.

During the long hours of the day, the German soldiers were rarely to be seen and the life of the island slowly reassumed its placid pattern. But with the coming of each dusk, the islanders were made sharply conscious of the reality of occupation. From their kitchens and their parlours they heard the harsh *staccato* of shouted commands and the rhythmic crunch of field boots on the roads. Peering out from behind lace curtains, they saw steel-helmeted squads of armed men marching in the ominous twilight. They saw men break off, singly and in pairs, to cross the darkening fields and stand guard over headland and cliff. During the hours of darkness, the men, women and children of Armorel stayed within the walls of their homes knowing, with a sense of bewildered resentment, that their beloved island was clasped in a loop of alien steel.

In that same afternoon of July the fourteenth, the Provost made his way to the Abbaye. A German orderly was weeding the drive and, as the Provost passed, the man looked up and said cheerfully:

"Good afternoon, sir."

"Good afternoon."

The Provost sighed. Despite the orderly's friendly greeting and obvious desire to practise his English on all and sundry, his occupation caused the Provost a feeling of dismay. One did not trouble to weed the drive of a house one was going to leave in the near future, and the simple act of pulling up grass and groundsel seemed to be the symbol of an inflexible purpose spread over an infinity of time.

The door was open and the Provost walked into the hall. In a side room, Sergeant Vogel was laboriously banging a typewriter. As soon as he saw the Provost, he strode angrily into the hall.

"It is your duty to knock at the door and to wait. You will not enter without permission. Is it understood?"

"Yes. It is understood." The Provost shrugged. "The Commandant ordered me to be here at three o'clock."

The sergeant glanced at his watch and grinned.

"You are punctual. You are not like Mister Lionel Fallaize. That is a good thing for you. Wait here."

The Provost sat down and studied his boots. The slow tick-tock of the grandfather clock was a melancholy sound to hear and the Provost's heart was heavy.

"The Commandant will see you now."

"Very well."

Captain Weiss was seated at his desk. As the Provost entered, he stood up.

"Good afternoon, *Monsieur le Provost*."

"Good afternoon, *Monsieur le Commandant*."

"Please sit down. May I offer you a Dutch cigar?"

"No, thank you."

"Well, then, please smoke your pipe if you wish." He sat down and lit a cigar, carefully watching the grey smoke. He said at last, "Well, my friend, we have been here for four days. I would like to know the general feeling of the island about our troops."

The Provost lifted one hand.

"They are *your* troops. You have answered your own question, monsieur."

"How so?"

"I explain myself badly. In no case have I heard a complaint. Your soldiers are quiet and courteous. I think they even wish to be friendly with the children." He paused. He said shrewdly, "Perhaps it is that they have orders to be friendly with the children so that, through them, your soldiers may gain the confidence and trust of their elders. I do not know. But if that were so, it would be an evil thing. No child should ever be used for a purpose, for any purpose. The people of Armorel are suspicious of you. Even if they were not so, it would be impossible for them to forget, even for a moment, that your men are German soldiers. In our eyes, they are not men. They are soldiers—and between your soldiers and us, there is . . . there is a space. I am sure that it will be so and remain so, no matter how long you stay."

"There is no question of our leaving, *Monsieur le Provost.* The Führer, Adolf Hitler, has said that the New Order will last for a thousand years."

"I am already an old man," said the Provost drily, "and I cannot see so far into the future as your Adolf Hitler. To me, a hundred years or a thousand is all one. But I know that the space will always remain between us."

"Surely we can bridge this space." Captain Weiss leaned forward. "Monsieur, I would do much to earn the confidence of your people."

"I believe you. But you will not be permitted to do so. Up to now, the wind has blown from the east and carried all before it. Soon the wind will blow from the west, and then everything will change for you."

"What do you mean? I am no islander to understand the winds."

The Provost's lined face was almost apologetic. He said slowly, "I mean that England is gathering her strength and that she will soon re-enter the fight. When that happens, you will be forced to control this island with . . . severity. When English soldiers scale our cliffs, you will not wish to give apples to the children. You will give bullets and not sweets. You will see."

Captain Weiss said shortly, "You are talking nonsense. England has been defeated. The war is over."

"Is it?" The Provost half smiled. "Then, if that is so, I have a request to make."

"Please make it."

"Food is scarce in Armorel and lavish in the sea, for this is the time of the year when the mackerel are in the tides. If the war is over, there can be no reason why we are forbidden to take our boats out. In the sea, around the coasts, there is a rich harvest ready for our hooks. We would like to reap this harvest—as we do in times of peace."

Captain Weiss looked at the old man. He was staring

humbly at his boots. Was there guile in his request? Was he seeking to trap the Commandant of Armorel in a verbal net? Captain Weiss thought not. He said, after a long pause:

"I would gladly give you permission to fish. But, once at sea, in their boats, what is there to prevent your able-bodied men from setting sail for England?"

The Provost looked up innocently.

"Why should you wish to prevent able-bodied men from reaching England? England is defeated and the war is over."

Captain Weiss stood up. He flung his leather belt round his waist and buckled it tightly, unconsciously stroking the holster that held his automatic. He put on his peaked cap and took up his gloves. He said icily:

"Your request is refused, *Monsieur le Provost.* It is one of my duties to make a report to Berlin on the pedigree stock of Armorel. We will begin by inspecting the Abbaye herd."

"Very well, *Monsieur le Commandant.*" He stood aside, his hat obsequiously in his hand, as Captain Weiss strode grimly out of his office.

In his office overlooking teeming Whitehall, Mr. Petherton sat back in his chair, put the tips of his fingers together and looked at Carruthers.

"Although it will be difficult, may I ask you for a few moments to dismiss this . . . er . . . isolated quadruped from your mind while I attempt to put her in her proper perspective. Thank you, Carruthers. Please sit down. You may smoke."

He gazed at the ceiling.

"You ask me to sanction an approach to the War Office. Let me merely outline *some* of the problems which confront my military colleagues as we sit here. The remnants of the British Army have been painfully withdrawn from the Continent of Europe. Ill-armed and half-trained, we in this island daily await the onslaught of our enemies by air, by sea and by land. At any moment now, London may become a smoking ruin; by next week, the Gestapo may be rounding up the Women's Institute of Sevenoaks and a Panzer Division drinking its beer in the licensed premises of Dover. That's how bad things are."

"I know that very well, sir. But may I put another point of view?"

"Go ahead."

"In this time of change and fear and confusion, Venus and her unborn calf represent stability and continuity. Because of that, and because these two, the one living and the other in the womb, are of incalculable value to the future of British pedigree breeding, I ask you, in all seriousness, if I may put this file to the War Office."

Mr. Petherton frowned. There could be no mistaking the sincerity that underlay this . . . this bizarre request. He said, hesitating:

"I am inexperienced in these matters. Suppose your Venus were to bear a female calf, surely the strain you so ardently desire would eventually be dissipated. For the preservation of the strain, a bull calf is essential. Am I correct?"

"You are, sir," he said eagerly. "But Venus will bear a bull calf. That is certain."

"So sex-determination also lies within your scope! You have solved the imponderable. You surprise me more and more."

"In Armorel, it has been known for centuries that if a calf is conceived when the tide is on the flood, it will be a bull. If a cow is served during an ebb tide, she will cast a heifer. With Venus nothing was left to chance. She was led to her mate on a day when a south-west wind packed a spring tide half-way up the cliffs of the island. A bull calf is sure."

Mr. Petherton gazed into the future over his spectacles.

"I will speak frankly. In my opinion, your enthusiasm has outrun your reason, Carruthers—and now you add superstition to your folly. To put this file officially to the War Office at this juncture is to invite ridicule. On the other hand," he said drily, "who am I to dissuade you from having unofficial—*and unrecorded*—conversations with the soldiery? In times like these, all things are possible and it may be that you will find someone in authority who is—yes, I shall use the word—who is as chivalrous as you are yourself."

"Thank you very much, sir."

Carruthers walked back to his office with a buoyant step. He glanced at his watch and picked up the telephone.

"War Office, please, on the direct line."

High over the roofs of London, the barrage balloons turned to shining sentries of gold in the declining sun.

Baptiste was an old man now, and his wife had been dead for many years. He lived alone in a cottage opposite the Abbaye, a cottage that had housed his father before him and his grandfather before that. For over fifty of his seventy-one years he had been cowman to the Abbaye herd and in that half-century of time no calf had been born whose pedigree, colour, markings and characteristics he didn't remember. Once, after deep thought, he had said to his master, the Suzerain:

"Monsieur, it is a very curious thing. Human beings are almost as different as cows," and this was how he saw his fellow-men.

His face was a sunburned maze of wrinkles and he had fisherman's eyes, blue, clear, very wide apart. Wise in weather and cropping, he was a deeply religious man, ending his infrequent sentences with a devout "*S'il plaît au Seigneur!*" The advent of the Germans to his beloved island was an event beyond his comprehension. He accepted the fact of their presence without either understanding or resentment. These strange men in uniform had come. One day—*s'il plaît au Seigneur*—they would go away.

He came to the door of his cottage and looked over the familiar fields of Armorel. There was not a breath of wind in the July afternoon and the air seemed to quiver in the heat of the sun. He knew, not by the hands of a clock but by instinct, the exact hour of the day. He put on his cap and began to trudge down to the lower meadow. The island needed rain for the long golden summer had burned the richness out of the grass. He passed the maize field, unconsciously recording the sturdy growth of the crop, saw that the oats were nearly ready for harvesting, ran his eye along the lines of roots, saw a gap in the wire netting. He would mend that this evening or the rabbits would be in among the young carrots. He wished the Suzerain were back in Armorel, he and his sister, Miss Nicola. It was lonely without them. *S'il plaît au Seigneur*, they would come back soon from the war and walk over the fields with him as they used to in friendship.

Baptiste entered the lower meadow and stopped, screwing up his eyes. Two men were standing by Venus, looking at her. One of them was his old friend the Provost and the other was a stranger, a man in uniform wearing a peaked cap. He must be one of the Germans. Baptiste's mouth hardened. The Germans had no right to examine Venus like that. He walked on, his stoop more pronounced, his old fingers clenched. As he approached, Venus looked up, blinking her soft, fringed eyes. Baptiste touched his cap to the Provost and stood there awkwardly. The Provost was obviously ill at ease.

"This is Baptiste, *Monsieur le Commandant*. He will be able to answer your questions."

The German officer gave Baptiste a swift, penetrating glance. "You are cowman at the Abbaye?"

"Yes, monsieur."

The German officer walked around Venus, looked at her critically from the other side. He approached her, peered into the amber depths of her ears, ran his hand along her straight back, felt the supple skin of her side with his fingers. Frowning, he put his hand on her udder, feeling its springy tissue. He stepped back. She was medium-sized and her shoulders were fine. She stood on straight, slender legs and she was deep, with well-sprung ribs to give ample heart room. Her hind legs were comfortably spread, the udder well forward and well up behind, the teats wide apart and evenly placed. Captain Weiss said slowly, "How old is this animal?"

Baptiste answered at once:

"Three years, eleven months and"—he counted on his fingers—"ten days, monsieur."

"So. And when is she due to calve?"

"In fourteen days, monsieur."

"I think she will be a day or two late." He took a Zeiss Ikon camera from his tunic pocket and focused it with the greatest care. Then he began to take pictures of Venus, walking round her, kneeling to get shots from every angle. Baptiste watched him with growing disquiet. This was no townsman. This was a man of knowledge and experience and the deliberation with which he photographed Venus filled Baptiste with a strange foreboding. He said in low, rumbling patois:

"*Monsieur le Provost*, I do not understand why——"

"Hush, Baptiste. Have patience. I will see that no harm comes to her."

Captain Weiss shut his camera, ran his hand once more along Venus's back and smiled.

"I was not always a soldier, *Monsieur le Provost.* Before the British declared war on Germany, I was a farmer and my herd of pedigree Friesians was renowned not only in Westphalia but throughout the Reich. This animal is as good a cow of her breed as I have ever seen. She is flawless. I think she will be of the greatest interest to the Reichsamt for Agriculture in Berlin. You will please instruct the cowman here to set out for me her pedigree, sire and dam back to great-grandparents and the same for the bull to whom she is in calf. I would also like her milk yield over a year and percentage of butter-fat content. Is it understood?"

"It is understood, *Monsieur le Commandant.*" His voice was troubled. "This cow is known to all of us and her calf could be very precious to us. May one ask——"

"You may ask nothing, *Monsieur le Provost.* If I were to answer you as a farmer, I would speak with a sympathy which, as an officer, I am unable to show. Please give your orders to . . . to what is his name? . . . to Baptiste."

"Monsieur, his English is bad. May I speak to him in patois?"

"Yes."

The Provost turned to Baptiste. He spoke rapidly:

"The Commandant requires the full pedigrees of Venus and of Mars. He also requires her milk yield and percentage of butter-fat. If you are clever, you will understand what to do."

The old man's eyes clouded with anxiety.

"But I can only tell the truth. Then what will happen to Venus?"

"You are a fool, my old friend. Give the figures to me and I will present them to the German officer. All will yet be well."

"*S'il plaît au Seigneur.*"

The Provost approached Captain Weiss humbly.

"I have given your orders. Baptiste understands."

"Good. Now we will look at the animals in the next field." He smiled. "They will suffer by comparison with this . . . this elegant goddess. Come."

"Very well, *Monsieur le Commandant.*"

The two men walked towards a gap in the grey stone wall. Baptiste put his hand on Venus's throat and began to stroke with tenderness. She stretched out her head and half closed her eyes in sleepy content. He began to talk to her, saying the same words over and over again:

"They will want to take you away to Germany but you will not go. You will not go to Germany. You will not go. You will not go. . . ."

CHAPTER SIX

VALENTINE

MAJOR VALENTINE MORLAND, ex-history don and bird-watcher and now an officer of no fixed military occupation, woke up in Brown's Hotel at seven o'clock in the morning of September the ninth and yawned luxuriously. It had been a fearful night.

He had arrived in London at about eight in the previous evening, to be welcomed by the banshee howling of air-raid sirens. The hours of darkness had resounded to a continuous cannonade and had been illuminated by the baleful glare of fire, for on this night Hermann Göring had first sent his massed squadrons to London. Valentine was sitting on the edge of his bed when the waiter came in with his tea and *The Times*. He looked red-eyed and strained and he put down the tray with a clatter.

"Good morning, sir. What a night."

"Yes. It was noisy."

" 'Noisy,' sir! They got it down in the East End mostly. About five hundred people killed." He used a dirty word to describe Hitler and apologized. "You've been away for a bit, haven't you, sir? Been on leave?"

"Yes. I've been on leave. Three weeks in the sunshine."

"Have a good time, sir?"

"Wonderful." He half-smiled. "Brighton was looking her best."

"They do say there's nowhere like good old Brighton. There's your paper, sir."

"Thank you so much."

Sitting on his bed while he drank his tea, Valentine read *The Times* systematically and with detachment. The personal column yielded its customary chorus of *cris du cœur*. A box number wanted to meet a water-diviner; the names of several officers were given—as was their new address—Oflag XII C; an ideal retreat (safety area) was offered to a gentlewoman; the perennial public schoolboy, who had a pleasing personality and who could drive a car, was prepared to go anywhere and do anything; a lady wanted to sell an electric hand vibrator—unwise in his generation, Valentine wondered why one should want to vibrate one's hands—and an anonymous recipient of favours gave expensive public thanks to Saint Jude. With a keen sense of loss, Valentine's eye scanned the column. Ah! There she was, bless her. A titled lady wished to dispose of her fur coat. All was well. England stood where England stood.

He turned to page four and, with narrowed eyes, read the headlines. Massed air attack on London. One hundred and seven raiders shot down. Widespread damage and many casualties. Fierce fires. Docks and industrial areas attacked. Sky lit up for miles.

What was the other side of the picture? It made thin reading.

The R.A.F. had attacked barges at Calais, Dunkirk and Boulogne. The Army in Egypt had been reinforced by the docking of a convoy. The Krupps works at Essen had been extensively damaged. The London cinemas promised "a busy week" and a new revue by Herbert Farjeon, called "In Town Again", seemed to Valentine to be specially designed as a personal welcome. He put down the paper and turned on his bath.

As the water gushed with a pleasant roar, Valentine turned out the pockets of the ghastly suit he had worn for the last three weeks. From the deep inside breast pocket he took a small loaded automatic pistol and spilled the cartridges out of the clip in the butt. The other pockets yielded little—for Valentine was a careful man. What they did yield was indicative of his paramilitary status. One Lisbon tram ticket and three sulphur matches; the telephone number of a certain Portuguese florist, written on the back of an envelope addressed to M. Georges Dufort, l'Avenida Palace Hotel, Lisbon; a receipted bill from the same establishment, also made out to M. Georges Dufort; a French passport in favour of the same M. Georges Dufort but which, oddly enough, bore a recognizable photograph of Major Valentine Morland, *en civile*. He folded the hotel bill carefully and put it in his wallet. It was extraordinary how parsimonious the Treasury could be about expenses. . . . In a burst of generosity, he decided not to present them with the tram ticket. It was at that moment that the telephone rang. He picked up the receiver. A voice barked one word at him:

"Valentine."

"Morland speaking. Who is that?"

"This is Uncle George."

Valentine glanced at his watch. It was twenty past seven. Did Uncle George ever go to sleep? He decided not. He said cautiously:

"Good morning, Uncle George."

"When did you get back?"

"Last night. Just in time for the Göring party."

"And is—all well?"

Valentine glanced at the spilled-out cartridges on his tea-tray. He had a sudden feeling of revulsion, a feeling almost of physical sickness. He said slowly:

"Oh, yes. All's well."

A man's face came between him and the cartridges. It was the face of a young man with one eye open. His skin was a fish-belly white and there were strong hairs in the blood of his wide nostrils. Valentine had flashed a torch on him before he had taken a lump of tungsten from his waistcoat pocket and walked away, his stomach heaving, to catch a tram back to the lighted streets and the teeming cafés of Estoril. He said again, "All's well."

"Fine. I want to see you, Valentine. I've got a job for you."

Valentine's heart sank.

"Another job—like the last one?"

"No." Uncle George's voice was a snarl. "Not in the least like the last one. I'm sending you, an able-bodied man, on the biggest piece of crack-brained nonsense of the war. That's all. Come in at eleven, to Room 057, War Office, Main Building."

"I will. Good-bye, Uncle George."

"And good-bye to you," said Uncle George grimly.

Valentine walked into the bathroom frowning. Now what lay before him?

At five to eleven, Valentine Morland showed his special pass to the security police at the staff entrance to the War Office and walked along a corridor on the ground floor to Room 057. He was in the uniform of a Major and he wore the lion and unicorn badge of General Service. He knocked and entered.

Uncle George was dictating to a middle-aged woman secretary. He was dressed as a Brigadier. Valentine saluted and Uncle George waved a vague hand. He said:

"Sit down. I won't be long. In the meantime, you might as well smoke and read this claptrap."

Valentine took the file and sat down. He lit a cigarette and began to read. When he had skimmed the contents of the file, he read it again with a growing sense of delighted incredulity. It took him some time to absorb, for the whole thesis, revealed in this bare War Office room, had an air of complete unreality. What had Room 057 of the War Office to do with the milk yield of a pedigree cow? How was this starting-place for so many dark adventures concerned with a distant calf still lying snug in the womb? Yet out of the neat paragraphs and precise phraseology, there stole a smell that curled sweetly in Valentine's nostrils. It was a good smell. The sea was in it and the coldness of spray snatched off the crests of breakers by a swinging wind; there was thyme in it, and clover and wood-smoke and human sweat. There was certainly human sweat. . . .

Valentine glanced at Uncle George. He wondered how many *soi-distant* nephews and nieces claimed relationship with this mysterious, extraordinary man whose real name Valentine didn't know. Some said that he was an ex-member of the Clydeside Police riot squad; some that he was the illegitimate son of Jack the Ripper; others said that he was a retired horse-butcher with a nostalgia for his old trade. Nobody knew, for he signed his infrequent written orders with indecipherable initials. Certain it was that he had an implacable hatred of Germans, that he enjoyed the confidence of the Chiefs of Staff and had the free run of the Treasury coffers. Valentine had met him in the first months of the war at a friend's house. "This," said his friend, "is my Uncle George." Uncle George had asked Valentine, then an infantry subaltern, if he was happy in his work and then gone on to say sardonically that he could offer several far more amusing ways of being killed than by being blown to pieces by an academic, anonymous bomb. Resentful of the enforced inactivity of the phoney war, Valentine had accepted gladly—and found himself to his dismay playing lethal games of chess with the members of Admiral Canaris' Abwehr in the back-streets of Europe's still neutral capitals. It was a long way from Killcanon Staircase to the bountiful cafés of Stockholm—and even further from the bird-haunted Hebrides to the slums of Madrid. Valentine comforted himself with the depressing knowledge that a shipload of manganese was as much an ingredient of victory as an infantry division and set out on his peculiar errands with what philosophy he could muster.

The middle-aged secretary stood up at last. Uncle George said, "Get all that stuff over to Baker Street for coding. Fast as you can."

"Very good, Uncle George."

Another adopted niece? *Quelle famille!*

"So you disposed of the boy friend."

"I did," said Valentine briefly. "I've written you a report of the whole nauseating business from beginning to end. Here it is."

Uncle George took the report and put it in his pocket.

"So you find the whole business nauseating. You should take a walk through the streets of Rotherhithe this morning, Valentine, and see the Union Jacks stuck up on the rubble. Then you might not be so squeamish about rubbing out one bastard in the Abwehr. Have you read that file?"

"I have."

"What do you think of it?"

"It pleases me profoundly."

"Why?"

"It's hard to explain. But in these days of battle, murder and sudden death, it is refreshing to know that at least one person, thank God, has had time to remember the ancient verities. At last I see a gleam of pure sanity in the horrid madhouse of Europe. That's why."

Uncle George looked at him with benevolent truculence.

"And now shall I tell you what I think of it?"

"No, don't. I know."

"Want to take it on?"

"Gladly."

"I was afraid you would."

"You knew perfectly well that I would. What help may I have?"

"Damn little. What do you want?"

"A first-class radio operator to begin with—and I know one. I used to watch birds with him. He's a Gordon sergeant named Alexander Forbes. And I want a lot of local information."

"Your best source of local information, as you call it, is a new and very hush-hush branch of Naval Intelligence, who hides its light under a bushel in Oxford. And the M.I. boys have dug you up a contact, some female battle-axe in the A.T.S. who used to live in Armorel. As bad luck would have it, this Amazon is stationed in North Wales, but she's being flown to London this morning. When she turns up, we'll make her your driver and she can take you to Oxford this afternoon. Pump her dry."

"I loathe being driven by women. They either crawl or drive at breakneck speed and they're for ever vanishing into Olde Worlde Teashops on mysterious female errands."

"My heart bleeds for you, Valentine. Combined Ops.—who appear to be as far divorced from reality as you are—are agog. I am perpetually confronted by middle-aged undergraduates who insist on climbing a sort of mental Martyrs' Memorial. Anyway these half-witted enthusiastic adolescents at Richmond Terrace have worked out a scheme for getting the blasted animal off the island. All you have to do, it appears, is to go to Armorel, bellow like a bull and she'll follow you like an ambitious chorus girl chasing a baronet." He stood up. He said savagely, "Little did I think when I took on this job that I'd have to ask one of my officers to be a bloody cowherd."

"I see myself more in the role of Saint George," said Valentine cheerfully.

"Then I suppose you see Venus as the King of Egypt's daughter. I must remind you that this lady has four legs and not two—and, by God, she doesn't wear black silk stockings. She doesn't even wear a——"

"Neither did the King of Egypt's daughter."

"Don't interrupt. You'd better get round to Combined Ops. straight away—and be back here at two o'clock. I'll warn Oxford that you're coming this afternoon. Do you want any money?"

"No. What would I want money for?"

"To buy yourself a milking-stool, a bucket and a straw to suck. And I'd planned a real job for you. Nobody wins wars with a pedigree calf and an armful of maize."

"I quite agree with you, Uncle George. But you

could win a peace with a pedigree calf and an armful of maize."

"Go to hell."

Valentine saluted.

As he walked out of the War Office he was conscious of a surge of buoyancy. Though the days were anxious and the nights full of fury, he knew that no country could lose whose Chiefs of Staff sanctioned a job like this at a time like this, and his heart already warmed to the far-away Venus and to the calf that stirred within her.

One got used to most things.

The Provost of Armorel hardly heard the bugle calls that awakened the German garrison in the morning, although the leaping notes echoed over the fields of the island. He was able to dismiss from his mind the sound of boots marching on the stony road and the shouted choruses of the German soldiers as they went in dusty columns from their barracks to their outposts on the cliffs. He got used to reading the smudged typewritten news bulletin that was posted every morning on the gate of the Abbaye for all to read and admire. This tissue of lies was of particular pleasure to him, for hidden under the innocent cover of his wife's Singer sewing machine was a receiving set at which he listened at a varying hour each day to the chaste tones of the B.B.C. announcers.

In the evening of September the ninth, the Provost walked up the weeded drive of the Abbaye. Captain

Weiss was in genial mood. So genial was he that he greeted the Provost in French.

"*Bonsoir, monsieur.*"

"Good evening, *Monsieur le Commandant.*"

Captain Weiss accepted the reproof in good part. Time would change many things.

"I have to-day received certain orders from the Commandant at Guernsey. You are aware that I sent a report to the Reichsamt for Agriculture in Berlin on the pedigree cattle of the island."

"Yes, monsieur, I am aware of this."

"What you do not know is that I also sent a special report on Venus de l'Abbaye and many photographs." He stopped. The Provost said nothing. "I am happy to tell you that the pedigree cow Venus de l'Abbaye is to be sent to Germany where she will bear her calf. Compensation—in marks—will be credited to the account of the absent Suzerain."

"But . . . but our Suzerain has not need for marks. He will not wish Venus to go to Germany—not for any number of marks. He will wish her to calve here—for the good of us all."

"I do not speak with two voices, but with one. Venus de l'Abbaye will go to Germany."

"Then it is my duty to tell you, monsieur, that I believe the island will resist you. If you steal . . . if you take Venus away from us, there will be trouble."

"Am I to understand," said Captain Weiss incredulously, "that I heard you use the word 'steal'?"

"It was the first word that came to my mind,

monsieur. We are a backward people in Armorel and lack refinements of speech. If one man takes by stealth or by force what belongs to another man, we call him a thief. We are no doubt very foolish. But we punish this dishonest man in the end. It is always so." He paused and then looked at Captain Weiss, directly and as an equal. "Like you, *Monsieur le Commandant*, I do not speak with two voices but with one. If you try to steal Venus, I repeat that the island will resist you."

Captain Weiss permitted himself the glimmer of a smile.

"So the island of Armorel will resist the Third Reich! The flea will resist the elephant . . ."

"There is an old saying, monsieur. Permit me to tell it to you. 'Patience, fleas! The night is long.' " He leaned forward and said with great sincerity, "I would not wish the men and women of Armorel to suffer for the sake of an animal. I ask you to let Venus remain here and thus make it possible for us to continue to live in peace."

Captain Weiss's mouth hardened.

"Until the time comes for Venus to go to Germany, she will be tethered in the top pasture under my eyes. That is all. You may go."

CHAPTER SEVEN

NICOLA

A FEW minutes before two, Valentine Morland returned to the War Office. He had had preliminary conversations with an enthusiastic Naval Commander at Combined Ops. and the scheme, as outlined by this genial sailor, seemed to him to be a reasonable one. The remains of a ham sandwich and an empty coffee cup stood on Uncle George's desk and his ashtray was full of cigarette ends.

"Well," he said, "does it make sense to you?"

"Yes. Given ordinary luck, we should get away with it."

"You don't want luck," said Uncle George, "what you want is a strait-jacket and a padded cell." He scribbled something on the cover of the file, and something else inside, threw it over to Valentine. "There you are. There's your passport to a German firing squad."

On the cover Uncle George had written "OPERATION VENUS". Inside was: "To Major Valentine Morland. For action. R.I.P."

"Your sense of humour is a little macabre," said Valentine, "but I see what you mean. . . ."

There was a knock on the door and a young woman

in A.T.S. uniform entered and saluted. Valentine glanced at her casually and returned to his file. Uncle George stood up. He said:

"Who are you?"

"Fallaize, sir. Reporting from North Wales."

"Oh, of course. You're the lady who used to live in Armorel."

"Yes, sir. But——"

"But nothing. Have you been allotted a staff car?"

"Yes, sir."

"Good. You will drive this officer to Oxford this afternoon and take orders from him until further notice. He will be at the staff entrance in five minutes."

"Very well, sir."

She saluted and left the room. Uncle George sat down again.

"So that's what I thought was going to be a battle-axe! All I can say is that if she's a battle-axe, I'd gladly be cut to pieces: if I thought she'd any brains I'd give her a job myself, but attractive women are invariably half-wits."

"Attractive, was she? I'm afraid I didn't notice. They all look alike to me in that ghastly uniform."

"There are times," said Uncle George, "when I despair for the continuance of the human race. I've told Oxford you're coming. Get what you can out of that young woman on the way and report to me here when you come back."

"I will, Uncle George."

As Valentine strode out of the War Office into Whitehall Place, the A.T.S. slid out of the driving seat of a Humber Snipe, saluted and opened the door to the back seat. Valentine acknowledged her salute. He saw a young woman of about twenty-one. She was dark, she had delicate, well-cut features and slim hands. All that he saw. He smiled. He said:

"Would you mind if I sat in the front seat beside you?" He hesitated. He added lamely, "Sitting in the back of a car always makes me feel sick."

"It is quite extraordinary, sir," she said with composure, "how many of my passengers seem to suffer from the same complaint. Do please sit beside me if you want to."

He sat down, angry not with himself but with the circumstances which had forced him to seem to make the dreary, moth-eaten advances of a philandering subaltern. He said curtly:

"I want to go to Oxford, please. To the School of Geography."

"Yes, sir. The Brigadier said that you wanted to go to Oxford."

"Do you know the way?"

"Oh, yes. Very well indeed. Would you like to go by Henley, which is the prettier way, or by Wycombe, which is the shorter?"

"By Wycombe, please."

"Very well, sir."

Buckingham Palace, Notting Hill Gate, the White City, Western Avenue, Gerrard's Cross . . . she drove sensitively and with skill, handling her car as if it were a blood-horse. They were sweeping up the incline of Beaconsfield before he spoke to her. He said in reluctant admiration:

"You drive very well."

"Beginner's luck, sir. I never even saw a motor-car until I was fourteen."

"Oh. Why not?"

"I lived in the island of Armorel. We're rather backward there, you know. No twentieth-century delights such as the tram, the motor-cycle, the fruit machine, the trolley-bus or the motor-car."

He half-smiled. She had unwittingly given him the lead he wanted. He lit a cigarette and stretched his legs.

"Armorel's one of the Channel Islands, isn't it?"

"Yes indeed. You must surely remember them from school. Jersey, Guernsey, Alderney, Sark—and Armorel."

"Of course. One remembers their cadence—like that of Henry the Eighth's wives."

"Exactly, sir." She began to recite. "Catherine of Aragon, Anne Boleyn——"

"I know history," he said drily. "May we please have a little geography? Tell me about Armorel."

"Armorel." Her dark eyes became luminous with interest. "Well, it's a small island, about two miles long and a mile and a half across. From the sea, it looks uninhabited, but it isn't. Something under three hundred people live there under the feudal but—I hope—benevolent rule of the Suzerain. Most of the islanders are either farmers or fishermen. There are a lot of odd customs and a lot of superstitions. For example, on one night of the year, the wells all turn into blood. That's what they say. But one thing is true. Armorel has magic in its soil. If it doesn't like you, the island won't have you. It will even call up a wind and throw a person it dislikes over the cliffs into the sea. A steep hill, called *Colline des Mouettes*, winds up to a plateau from the harbour. At the north of the island there's a passage between the rocks called *Le Couloir du Diable*—that means the Devil's Passage—and it's the grave of many ships."

"Please go on. You interest me very much."

"With geography? Or would you prefer flora and fauna?"

"Geography, please."

"In asking me to tell you about Armorel, you are unlocking the fountains of my heart." She laughed, and suddenly stopped laughing. "It's odd how fond you can get of a few distant acres, but there it is." She shook her head. "Well, the cliffs are very high and there's only one harbour although I know a dozen landing places. There are two languages, English and our own patois."

"Do you speak it?"

"Me?" She looked at him, incredulous at his question. "Of course I do." For some minutes she drove in silence. "Is there anything else you'd like to know about Armorel?"

"Yes, there is," he said carefully. "Tell me about a place called *La Pointe de Joie*."

"*Pointe de Joie!* I know it very well. My cousin Lionel and I used always to swim there when we were little. You go past the Abbaye, along a good road and then it becomes a path that leads down to the sea. There used to be a landing-place there because there's deep water, but it isn't used any more except in an emergency." She wrinkled her forehead. "Do tell me, sir, why are you interested in the *Pointe de Joie*?"

He evaded her question.

"When you leave this good road of yours, is the path down to the sea very steep?"

"No, not very. It's stony and it runs between bracken and blackberry bushes. Heavens, I could walk it blindfolded on the darkest night."

"Could you? And you wouldn't fall and cut your knees?"

"No. I wouldn't even slip."

Valentine gazed ahead, busy with his own thoughts. After a long time he said casually:

"When did you get away?"

"I didn't get away. When the war began my brother and I just came away. He joined the Army and I joined the A.T.S. They made me into a cook—and their digestions have suffered ever since. But getting away was as simple as that—then."

"Are your parents still there?"

"My mother died a long time ago and my father was accidentally drowned in 1938. There's only my brother and me." There was a long pause. She said in a curiously flat voice, looking straight ahead, "That's not quite true. I have a cousin who stayed on in Armorel: he's the one I used to swim with off the *Pointe de Joie*. He's a painter . . . and . . . and in spite of the fact that the Germans walk our fields, Lionel doesn't see the war as my brother and I see it."

"Tell me more about your cousin Lionel."

"I . . . I haven't seen him or heard of him since I left Armorel. I know nothing of him—now."

"Never mind. Here's Oxford. Tell me about what you used to know of him on the way home."

The Humber Snipe turned into Parks Road, drew up outside the School of Geography. Arrived at the entrance, Valentine got out. He said formally:

"I shall be about an hour. Would you like to have some tea and be back here at five? By the way, may I know your name?"

She replied with equal formality:

"Thank you very much, sir. My name is Fallaize, Nicola Fallaize."

"Right, Miss Fallaize. Five o'clock, then."

Valentine showed his pass to the Royal Marine sentry and was escorted to an outer office through which he had to walk before entering the room of Colonel Nigel Dunn, Commandant of the Department. A secretary looked at him innocently and, as soon as Colonel Dunn's door closed, picked up her telephone.

"War Office please. Room 057. Oh, hullo. Uncle George? Oxford here. Your man has just come. Shall I describe him? He's a Major, wearing uniform with General Service badges. Age about twenty-eight.

Clean-shaven, grey eyes, slightly vague manner, springy walk. Right? Thank you so much. Good-bye, Uncle George."

She put down the receiver, tapped on Colonel Dunn's door. She said meaningly: "I have checked the typescript, sir. It is quite in order."

"Thank you." Colonel Dunn smiled and opened his cigarette-case. "Well, Morland, I gather that you are in search of some local colour on the island of Armorel. I've asked my chaps to dig you out maps and charts and any holiday snapshots they've got. Uncle George tells me that he's put you on to a female battle-axe who knows the island well."

"Yes, sir. She's an A.T.S. driver—and more like a stiletto than a battle-axe."

"Useful?"

"Very. Full of topography, nostalgia and superstition."

"Good. Well, we at this end are looking for another contact for you, an odd character called 'Trawler' Langley. He is reputed to know these waters as well as anybody alive. Trouble is we can't find him. He hasn't been home for thirty-six hours and his landlady is getting worried. She thinks he may have been caught in last night's blitz, but I doubt it. He's a man with an inordinate thirst and the only thing likely to kill him is cirrhosis of the liver. The search continues." He rang a bell and a short, smiling Naval officer came into the room. "Oh, Bill, this is Morland, from the War Office, who's interested in Armorel. Help him all you can, will you? Come and see me again before you go, Morland."

"Right, sir."

As they walked along the passage, the Naval officer said with interest:

"Who's the popsy?"

"The popsy? Oh, you mean my driver. She's just a contact. Believe it or not, she's a cook as well."

"I know nothing of her cooking but what a contact! Well, I've got out a lot of stuff for you. . . ."

Nicola Fallaize drove slowly along the Broad, parked her car outside St. John's and walked across to the Randolph for tea. For a while she glanced leisurely at last week's *Tatler*, not so much out of interest in its polished pages as to divert the ardour of a young man in battle-dress with NORWAY on his shoulder and conquest in his eyes. When he left in despondent search of other game, she put down the paper, yawned and considered the surprising sequence of events since the sun had risen over her barrack room in North Wales.

At a quarter-past eight she had been in overalls and wooden clogs swabbing out the sergeants' mess kitchen and pondering the inevitability of roast beef and two veg., when she had been summoned to the presence of her Junior Commander, a hatchet-faced female with eyes like gimlets and the skin of a dyspeptic.

"Fallaize," she had said, "I have received an immediate posting order for you, direct from the War Office itself. It appears that you are to be flown—

flown, Fallaize—to London at once, where you are to report to the M.T. company to pick up a Staff car and then to Room 057, the War Office, 'for special duty'." She had sat back with an Arctic smile and gone on in a voice tinged with lemon juice. "Possibly you can explain, Fallaize, why a junior member of the section should be singled out for aeroplane jaunts to London. Can it have some connection with the fact that you spent your last leave in London with"—she turned over some papers—"with your Aunt Heloise in Sloane Street? Or is it possible that your 'Aunt Heloise' is a member of the General Staff with power to order your comings and goings? If your driving is as good as your cooking, I fear for the future."

"I know nothing of it, ma'am. I am as bewildered as you are. But I can drive."

"I hear what you say. Please pack up your things. I shall have you driven to the airport—by yourself."

Feeling slightly like the bacillus of a particularly noisome skin disease, Nicola was driven to the air-strip and handed over to the exuberant hands of a pilot officer who regarded the journey as a godsend, having nocturnal plans of his own for London. She flew high over the Welsh mountains and the cobweb fields of the Midlands, evaded the pilot officer with practised skill at the discreet airfield in Bedfordshire when they landed, and was driven to London in the unaccustomed grandeur of a staff car. Then she reported to the War Office M.T. Company, was allotted a Humber Snipe, ate a mystified sandwich and drove to Whitehall.

And now—Oxford.

That the reason for her abrupt flight to London was somehow concerned with Armorel was sure. She had said that to speak of the island unlocked the fountains of her heart. She had said it lightly, smiling as she used the phrase. But it was not altogether untrue. The island and its fields were dear to her. Sitting in the lounge of the Randolph, she took that road that led past the Abbaye, the road that became a path that went down to the *Pointe de Joie*. She did not walk the path alone.

It was, she supposed, inevitable that she should have fallen in love with her cousin Lionel. He'd always been there and there were few adventures of childhood that they had not shared. She saw him clearly as he had been in those days, a thin, restless little boy, intolerant of criticism. It was he who had always been the leader of their dangerous expeditions and she had willingly followed where he led. It was Lionel who knew the way to the seagulls' most precarious nests, and it was Lionel who chose a day to climb the tempestuous cliffs when the trees of Armorel were bent back before a screaming gale. Careless of the tide and the weather, he had not persuaded but commanded her to sail with him when he drove a leaky dinghy through the leaping spray of the *Couloir du Diable*, a feat which earned for her not only a soaking but the promise of pneumonia and a well-deserved, old-fashioned nursery spanking from her father. Then the eager little boy with scarred knees had been sent away to school in England, and she had roamed the island in the happy but less stimulating society of her brother Luke.

In the holidays they had met joyously, each of them expecting to recapture the old, careless magic of the windy cliffs. But something seemed to have changed. As they grew up, Lionel had become more impatient, more dominating and she, to her bewilderment, more secretive. She had no longer been prepared to wade light-heartedly among the salt pools in torn knickers and a tight jersey. She wouldn't even wear a jersey any more when Lionel was with her, because it made her acutely self-conscious when he looked at her with that new intensity. Swimming was different too. She always contrived to undress far away from him, and to enter and leave the water by herself. She was dismayed and a little frightened by the onrush of adolescence and withdrew into a quiet place where she could dwell alone. Sometimes she longed passionately to be able to shut her eyes and leap back into the simplicities of childhood; but, at other times, she was conscious of a new and exciting dignity, a sense of mounting awareness that sprang from the changing chemistry within her. They had been difficult days, and she was always glad and at peace when he went away. But not for long.

When she, too, went away to school in England they wrote to each other during term time. Lionel's letters were pompous and discursive, usually exploding into violence on the last page. He wrote long, wordy dissertations on pre-Raphaelite painting, war, primitive sculpture and Catholicism. His hatreds were as sharp as they were variable, and everything he wrote was signed in the grand manner with the single, self-conscious initial "L". For a while Nicola attempted to keep up with him, compiling laborious essays on the ballet, equal pay for equal work and the poems of François Villon. These effusions, checked for spelling with the *New English Dictionary*, were signed by the letter "N". Then she conceived a passion for the swimming mistress and, until that brief tornado blew itself out, Lionel's letters remained unanswered. . . .

The waiter in the Randolph asked her politely if she would like some more buttered toast. With an effort she jerked herself back from the mists of Armorel to the reality of Oxford in 1940. She shook her head. No, thank you. No more. He went away. Nicola darted gladly back across the seas to her island and to its rippling winds.

She stirred uneasily. Where was Lionel now? Was he still painting his tortured pictures—by courtesy of Adolf Hitler? Was he in a German concentration camp or was he dead? Where was the little boy with the cut knees who had been her playmate, the pompous public schoolboy who had suddenly become an undergraduate who, by his physical presence, had forced on her the terrifying timidities of a young girl inarticulately in love. She supposed now that she had always loved him, even in the blind years, and at long last, in the final spring of peace, that love had become realized.

It had come about in a curious way. On her way back from a farm overlooking the *Macquereau,* she had passed Lionel's house. A light had been on in the studio and she had walked in unceremoniously as she had done a thousand times before. He had been sitting on the floor, staring at a new canvas, a confection of skulls and misshapen men. He had said, tormented by grief and by doubt:

"Hullo, Nicola. What do you think of that?"

"What is it?"

"It's called 'Vibrations on a theme'."

"Oh."

The painting was hideous. There had been nothing other than "Oh" for her to say. At last he had stood up and said to her, out of nothing:

"If a war comes, what will you do?"

She had shrugged. "Go to it, I suppose. I can't do much. I'm a woman."

"I know you're a woman. By God, I know you're a woman."

She had looked at him quickly, startled by his vehemence. Then there had been a long silence between them, a petrified silence in which Nicola had heard no sound in the world except the thumping of her own heart. He had said, out loud in words, a thing of which, in his turbulent society, she had become increasingly conscious. Until now she had been aware of a slight sense of guilt, but that was gone utterly, for she knew that she was no longer alone in the realization of her own maturity.

"So you don't like my painting?"

"I think it's terrible."

"Then you're a fool." He had looked for a long time at nothing, then he had said in a blurred voice quite unlike his own, "I like you very much, Nicola."

"And I you."

"I don't want you to go to the war. Can't you see that it's only if people like you and me, who are young and who have their lives before them, make a stand that the vile old men who want to destroy us can themselves be destroyed? Can't you see that——?"

No. She couldn't see. She could only see that the man who loved her was talking, talking, talking, when surely he should take her in his arms. She realized with foreboding in that transparent moment that she was one forever with this gentle, tempestuous man, whose mother, whose lover and whose child she knew herself to be.

A few weeks had been left to them. The April winds dropped, the daffodils withered and the roses in the Abbaye garden opened their petals to the young summer sun. Lionel and Nicola walked the roads, the paths and the pastures of Armorel. Sometimes they walked hand in hand like children, more often they were content separately to be together. Even their quarrels were veined with gentleness and their thoughts and their blood flowed in harmony. There was a strange, remote courtship and when the storm of war broke, she knew that she would have to go away and that he would have to stay. She had bidden him a gay good-bye, though her heart was cracking.

"I'm off to be a hired assassin, Lion. When I come back, you must paint me in my uniform."

"I want to come with you. But I can't."

"Of course you can't. I see that."

"Bless you, Nicky. Come back soon from your bloody war."

"I will."

It didn't matter. She was bound to him, hand, foot and heart.

"May I give you your bill, madam?"

"Please do."

Nicola looked at her watch. It was a quarter to five. She had not had any realization of the passage of time. She paid her bill, walked out into the sunshine, started her car, drove to the School of Geography.

At the hour, she heard with delight coveys of melody start up and take flight into the summer sky from the singing belfries of Oxford. Before the echoes of that sweet chiming were lost in the steeps, Nicola was back in Armorel. She was following Lionel up the rickety ladder to the church tower where the ancient bell hung motionless. Together they traced the inscription engraved on its resonant dusty sides:

Venez, montez à la Maison éternelle.

CHAPTER EIGHT

VENEZ, MONTEZ . . .

VALENTINE MORLAND walked thoughtfully back to Colonel Dunn's office. The Colonel was looking at a little pile of what appeared to be shingle on his desk. He smiled at Valentine's obvious curiosity.

"What do you think this is, Morland?"

"Looks to me like a handful of shingle, sir."

"It is a handful of shingle. It was taken at some hour between midnight and dawn last night from a French beach by one of my chaps, who went out in a small boat. Odd to think that a man risked his life to grab a handful of small stones, isn't it?"

"But what's it for?"

Colonel Dunn swept the pile carefully into an envelope and sealed it.

"One day, Morland, the British Army will land again on the European shore. It would be sad indeed if our armoured vehicles were to be bogged down by ignorance of the physical composition of the beach." He sat back. "Well, have you got what you want on Armorel?"

"Yes. You've been most helpful."

"Good. Well, that's the best we can do for you—pending our finding the redoubtable 'Trawler' Langley.

I think we've got a line on him. Where can I find you by telephone to-night in case I want you?"

"I'm living at Brown's Hotel. And I thought I'd dine at the Epicure in Soho."

"Good. If anything happens I'll ring you there. Best of luck on your trip. Bring me back a handful of shingle—and keep your feet dry."

"Hope so, sir. Good-bye."

Valentine went out to the waiting car. Nicola opened the front door. He said politely:

"Sorry I had to keep you waiting. You've had some tea?"

"I have indeed. With hot buttered toast."

"Fine. Well, off we go to London—and to-night's display of *furor teutonicus*."

"Meaning the blitz?"

"Exactly. Meaning the blitz." The car drove up the Banbury Road, turned right into the by-pass. Valentine said casually: "You were going to tell me about your cousin who stayed in Armorel. What's his name . . . something beginning with an 'L'?"

"His name is Lionel. I told you on the way down that he's a painter. I . . . I don't think I want to talk about Lionel much."

Valentine glanced at her. She was gazing straight ahead. He had time to see how very bright her eyes were, and how delicate the modelling of her features. She glanced at him quickly, almost defensively. She said:

"But I'll tell you anything else you want to know about Armorel."

"Tell me about your cattle."

"Our cattle!" She frowned and then laughed. "What a curious question. As a matter of fact we're rather smug about our cows. They're pedigree Guernseys and a lot of them are Advance Register."

"What does that mean?"

"It's a bit complicated. It means that they have to show an average milk yield of a prodigious number of gallons over a complete year and that their milk has to have a high percentage of butter-fat. When a cow applies, as it were, for membership of this exclusive Advance Register she's put 'on test'. It's a sort of bovine Guards Club—with a probationary period."

"I see. The real point is, are they nice, quiet, obedient cows?"

She smiled. "Very nice, very quiet and most obedient. Just like the Guards. Why?"

"I only wondered."

Silence settled between them. As they swept on to London, Valentine pondered deeply on the *minutiæ* of war. One man set sail under cover of night to collect a few ounces of revealing gravel from the enemy-occupied shore; a pilot braved flak and fighter to take one significant photograph of one significant building; here was he, an able-bodied man, making exhaustive inquiries into the temperament of the pedigree Guernsey cow. The odd thing was that it all made sense and that this seemingly unrelated bric-à-brac fitted into the grand mosaic of the battle.

Captain Weiss walked in the evening of that same day to inspect the layout of the minefield that was to be sown in the fields above the *Pointe de Joie*. On his way back, he was pleased to see Lionel Fallaize walking ahead. He quickened his pace and caught up with him at the bend of the road. Weiss saluted punctiliously and greeted him with a smile.

"Good evening, Mr. Fallaize."

"Good evening."

"May I walk a little way with you?"

"You are lord of all you survey. Who am I to stop you walking where and with whom you like?"

"You are not very gracious, Mr. Fallaize."

Lionel stopped and frowned. He said frankly:

"No, I'm not. I'm sorry. Do walk with me."

At a slow pace they walked in step in the direction of the Abbaye. Captain Weiss said in a friendly voice:

"How goes the painting?"

Lionel shrugged. He said bitterly:

"One of the prerequisites of decent work is a sense of freedom. One can hardly say that that obtains in Armorel."

"The occupation of the island is a military necessity, forced upon us by England's declaration of war. I think you will agree that I have tried to make our presence as unobtrusive as possible."

"Yes. I think that you have done your best. But can't you see that one is conscious all the time of the fact of imprisonment? It doesn't matter a damn whether the cell bars are visible or invisible. They are there. The dawn and the sunset, even the curl of the waves, have become military secrets. You ask me how my painting is going. It has hardened and become angular. The power to soften and to make my work gentle has gone from my fingers. I paint cells, Captain Weiss, from within a cell."

"I am trying to understand you, Mr. Fallaize." He stopped and looked around. "Here, on the plateau where you can move freely, there are a thousand beautiful things to paint. Look at the sweep of that pasture. It is as rounded and as smooth as the thigh of a woman. Look at those seagulls and how they ride the wind. These things are surely subjects for your brush—not the prison bars of England's making."

"If I tried to paint that field, it would become the exercise yard of a jail. If I painted the gulls, they would be seen through an iron trellis."

"A pity. We are nearly at the Abbaye. Would you care to join me in a glass of beer in the Mess?"

"Please don't think me discourteous if I say no. In an atmosphere of Luegers and uniforms, your beer would be sour in my mouth."

Captain Weiss smiled.

"You are consistent, Mr. Fallaize. Your principles are stronger than your thirst and that I admire. Please accompany me to my office."

"Is this a command?"

"Yes. It is a command."

They walked up the drive. Every weed, every tuft of grass had been removed and the edges had been meticulously trimmed. Everything was as spick and span as a front garden in Surbiton. The sentry at the door sprang to attention, saluted like a marionette. With an air of distaste, Lionel followed Captain Weiss into the hall he knew so well. Suddenly he stopped dead. He looked up the wide staircase. He did not know nor could he ever know what strange telepathy prompted that eager glance. In silence he heard his own voice calling, "Nicola." He heard her bedroom door bang and her step on the landing. She came to the landing and leaned over the banisters. She was wearing a flowered linen dress with a tight bodice and a wide, flowing skirt. She said, "It's a grand morning. Where shall we go?" and he knew that in a moment, now, she would run down the stairs and that they would go out together into the morning and climb the rickety ladder to the church tower. . . . He shook his head. Before his startled eyes, her presence dissolved and vanished as swiftly as it had come. He drew a deep breath and walked into Captain Weiss's office.

"Please sit down, Mr. Fallaize." He frowned. "You look . . . you look as if you had seen a ghost."

"I have."

Captain Weiss chuckled. "I have always known you to be a complex character. In the next edition of *Who's Who* you must add on to the study of Serbian pottery the fact that you are psychic." He wrote a few lines on a sheet of official paper, blotted it and sat back in his chair, the tips of his fingers together.

"Mr. Fallaize," he said, "you may or may not be

surprised to learn that you have been very carefully watched. Since we have been here, no movement of yours has been unrecorded. I now believe your story. I believe you to be what you say you are—an artist with no activity other than painting. Because of this, I have decided to give you permission to move freely about Armorel." He handed the sheet of paper to Lionel. "Paint your dawns and your sunsets where you like and at what hour you like. That is your passport. With that, no sentry will question your comings and goings."

Lionel read the few lines. It was, as Weiss had said, a passport—a passport to freedom. He stood up and put the letter on Weiss's desk.

"You're a decent chap, Weiss. But I can't accept this."

"It is because you, too, are a decent chap that I give it to you. Why can't you accept it?"

Lionel looked at him steadily.

"Because I am, first of all, an islander of Armorel. After that, I am a painter. I am unwilling to be privileged above my friends. Free us all—and I will gladly paint you a picture—of a seagull without a black network of bars. Sorry, Weiss, but that's how it is. In the meantime, I must be content with my diagonals and right angles. Good night to you."

Mr. Fallaize had gone. The white oblong of paper lay unfolded and uncreased on Captain Weiss's desk. He looked at it absent-mindedly, reading the curt, generous sentences over and over again. In the textbook on procedure to be followed in the case of military occupation of enemy territory, there was no section, no paragraph which could help him in a situation like this. Could it be that the all-seeing and omnipotent Führer had forgotten something? He picked up the sheet of paper and read it again. A tiny flicker of anger was suddenly fanned into flame. Savagely he tore the letter into a thousand pieces, twisting the scraps of paper in his fingers, muttering. He rang a bell violently and his Adjutant came hurrying in.

"*Herr Hauptmann.*"

Captain Weiss spoke harshly in German.

"You will continue to watch Mr. Fallaize. If he transgresses our laws in the slightest way, even innocently or by accident, he is to be arrested and brought to me immediately. You understand? He is to be watched night and day."

"*Jawohl, Herr Hauptmann.*"

Lionel Fallaize walked out of the Abbaye. The sentry saluted him and he acknowledged the courtesy with embarrassment. At the Abbaye gate he hesitated. His home, where he intended to go, lay to the right. As if guided by a force beyond his control, he turned to the left. He made his way to the little square of grass that lay like an island between the converging gravel paths to the church. He leaned against the old stone wall that enclosed the cemetery where so many men and women of his name lay at peace. He looked up at the church tower, solid and strong against the darkening sky. To-morrow at the rising of the sun, the motionless bell that hung there would waken and swing and ring. To-morrow it would peal over pasture and plough, over minefield and sentry and cliff. It would peal until its echoes were lost in the windy distances beyond the locked shores of Armorel . . . and each chime of that resonant bell would thunder its summons and its reveille into the sky.

Venez, montez à la Maison éternelle. . . .

CHAPTER NINE

THE BLOOD OF KINGS

IT was after seven o'clock when the Humber Snipe drew up outside the Staff entrance to the War Office. There were few people in the darkening streets and over the roofs of the vast, stricken city there was an air of tension as London waited for the malice of the night.

Valentine got out of the car stiffly. Standing on the pavement, he looked up at the ominous sky. He said, speaking with slight embarrassment:

"Thank you so much for all you've told me." He hesitated. "I suppose you wouldn't care to dine with me to-night. Or would you? By the way, my name's Morland, Valentine Morland."

"Oh, I know all about that. You were a history don at St. Jude's and you used to watch birds in the Hebrides. I danced with you two years ago at Commem and you didn't notice me at all. Very chastening it was, too, because I'd spent a lot more than I could afford on a frock that was specially designed to knock dons sideways."

"You must think me very rude."

"Not at all. I think your mind is on higher things—on the *Pointe de Joie* at Armorel, for example." She laughed. "Will you tell me one thing—to satisfy my quite shameless feminine curiosity?"

"Certainly, if I can."

"Is this what might be called a normal invitation, or is it given because you want to go on finding out more about the topography—and cows—of Armorel?"

"You ask the most difficult things, but I'll answer you faithfully. I admit that the idea first came to me as a means for further . . . interrogation. But that was a long time ago, before we even left Oxford. Now you may take it that it is what you call 'a normal invitation'. In other words," he said carefully, "I would ask you to dine even if you had never been nearer Armorel than Waterloo Station. Definitely."

"In that case," she said with composure, "I'd love to come. Where and when? I've got to put this car away and then I'm going to my aunt's house in Sloane Street where I'm staying. I'd like time to have a bath and get out of this ghastly uniform. But I could meet you by, say, half-past eight. Would that be too late?"

"No, that wouldn't be too late. Do you know the Epicure in Soho, in Gerrard Street? It's quiet and the man who runs it is a friend of mine with a beard and a limp. The cooking is admirable and the cellar of claret magnificent. The Blood of Kings at half a crown a bottle. Or would you prefer somewhere with a band and some coons?"

"No band and no coons, thank you. The Blood of Kings at half a crown a bottle will do. Half-past eight at the Epicure. *Au revoir.*"

"*Au revoir.*"

The Humber Snipe drove along Whitehall Place as Valentine strode into the War Office.

"Well," said Uncle George, "how did you get on?"

"Splendidly. I'm beginning to think I was born on Armorel—in a calving byre and brought up on salt clover."

"How about that young woman, the A.T.S. cook? Was she any good to you?"

"Miss Fallaize is a living *Encyclopædia Armoreliana.* There seems to be practically nothing she doesn't know about the island."

"So I should damn well hope." He sat back and scowled. "Queer how the M.I. boys missed the obvious. I put over an inquiry for fun the other day asking for any dope they had on Adolf Schickelgruber and the answer came back 'Nothing known', so it's hardly surprising that they failed to identify your island-born brunette."

"Who is she?" said Valentine with interest.

"You are moving in high society, Valentine. Nicola Fallaize is the daughter of the late Suzerain of Armorel and the sister of the reigning one—who, by the way, is a bearded thug in Archie Wavell's Long Range Desert Group. He's no good to us because he's too far away. But, by God, the young woman's useful. Exit the A.T.S. incinerator of beef, in fact, and enter a female mediæval cowherd whose brother actually bred the blasted animal. The thing's rapidly becoming a family party. Where is she now, the heifer, not the cow?"

"Miss Fallaize is putting her car away. Then we're meeting for dinner."

"Are you?" He sat back with a wicked grin and copied Valentine's voice. "Do they all still 'look alike in that ghastly uniform'? By the way, she's got a cousin on the island called Lionel Fallaize, some long-haired pacifist painter. I'd steer clear of him, if I were you. But as regards the wench herself, you may go the limit."

"Thanks very much."

"Not at all. Help yourself. Get her to run you up an omelette *aux fines herbes* and tell her everything. I've sent for your Gordon Highlander radio operator and he's coming south from Scotland to-night. Come and see me to-morrow morning if you both survive to-night's blitz. Good night to you."

"And good night to you, Uncle George." He looked hard at the Brigadier. "One thing. If you think I'm taking that young woman or any other young woman with me to Armorel you're making a great mistake."

"Am I? Off you go to dinner and don't start bellowing like a bull—yet. Good night."

"Good night. But I mean what I say."

Promptly at half-past eight, Valentine sat in the bar of the Epicure fooling with a gin and Dubonnet and reading the *Evening News*. Every now and again he glanced over his paper at the door and at his watch. It was twenty to nine before the door opened and a young woman walked in alone. Valentine looked at her casually and returned to page three. She looked round the bar and came over to where he waited.

"Hullo," she said. "I'm sorry but I'm ten minutes late."

Valentine scrambled to his feet and gazed at her with a look of utter unbelief. The A.T.S. girl who had taken him to Oxford had vanished into thin air. In her place stood a girl in a frock of dark green taffeta in the texture of which there was a glint of gold. A single string of pearls shone round her neck. Her fair hair, which had been so severely gathered under her disfiguring cap, now hung to her shoulders. It had been brushed back to reveal, set in the lobes of her ears, two tiny Chinese fish of beaten silver, their scales ingeniously overlapping. Her lips that had been so formal were now full, red and mobile and her skin was warm with youth. Most startling of all was the change in her manner. She had become a completely different person. Even the movements of her hands and the carriage of her body were different. He said with an engaging blend of the schoolboy and the scholar:

"Golly! What a metamorphosis."

"This is my battledress Number Two."

"Is this the one . . . that was designed to knock dons sideways?"

She shook her head. "No. I'm saving that one up."

"Heaven preserve me from it. I'm reeling already. What may I order you to drink?"

"I'd love a dry Martini."

"You shall have it. I hope you haven't got to hurry home or anything. I've got several things to talk to you about after dinner."

"I thought you might."

He said slowly, "May I tell you that you look like who you are."

"Oh?"

"Yes. You look like the Princess of Armorel." He paused. "You . . . you might have told me."

"You didn't ask. Anyway, I think that you are more interested in things than you are in persons."

"Am I?" He laughed. "I used to be. I'd like to suggest *pâté maison*, followed by Coq au vin and a bottle of Pontet Canet. Would you like that?"

"Very much indeed. The Blood of Kings, *not* at half a crown a bottle. By the time coffee comes, I'll be able to give you a positively lyrical description of the *Pointe de Joie*."

As she lifted her dry Martini, he looked for the first time at her left hand. His glance was swift and, to his surprise, reassuring.

The long September evening was fading into darkness and a cool wind breathed in the bracken of the *Pointe de Joie*. Silhouetted against the still luminous breast of the sea, the jet-black figure of a German sentry stood absolutely immobile. There was a deep sense of the ominous in his very immobility, in his armed, alert and patient watchfulness.

At the moment when Valentine and Nicola were starting coffee, the *maître d'hôtel* came limping across to their table. He said:

"Excuse me, Major. There is a personal call on the telephone for you—from Oxford."

Valentine stood up. He said to Nicola, "I'm so sorry. Back in a minute."

He walked quickly to the telephone box, took up the receiver. "Morland here."

Colonel Dunn's voice spoke curtly from Oxford.

"Do forgive me for interrupting your dinner party, but we've located the gentleman whose name I gave you this afternoon. You know who I mean."

"I do, sir."

Colonel Dunn chuckled.

"Well, it appears that he has been having one of his periodic blinds—which are invariably followed by a night in the cells and by public repentance. If you attend Bow Street Police Court at opening time, as it were, to-morrow morning, you'll catch him on the rebound."

"How will I know him?"

"You can't miss him. He's got a huge black beard. Let me know when you've had a talk to him and then send him down to us for briefing. Right?"

"Right, sir. Good night to you."

"Good night."

Valentine went back to his table. He looked at Nicola, frowning. After a moment he said:

"Do you know a man named 'Trawler' Langley?"

" 'Trawler'! Of course I know 'Trawler'." Her surprise at his question was clear.

"Tell me about him."

"You do ask the oddest questions. You dart from road surfaces to cows and now to local celebrities." She wrinkled her forehead. "Trawler Langley is the modern equivalent of the Elizabethan pirate. He has lived in the islands all his life and he's got an almost uncanny knowledge of our not very calm seas. I used to sail with him sometimes when no one was looking. He's a robust character, full of rum, ribaldry and laughter. I suppose," she said with a sigh, "that if I ask you why you're interested in Trawler, you'll neatly change the conversation."

"No, I won't." He paused. "Are you wide awake?"

"Very much so."

"Good." He looked at her very solemnly. "Do you know what the word 'security' means?"

"It means keeping things secret."

"True. In this case, it means a lot more than that. It means the difference between freedom and captivity, even between life and death, to a number of people."

"You may trust me absolutely."

"I know it. Because not only I but other people trust you absolutely. I'm now going to tell you a story. It is a true story—or, I should say, it will be. Every story has a name and the name of this one, which will have as its background the *Pointe de Joie* at Armorel, is 'Operation Venus'. . . ."

In the parlour of his cottage, the Provost sat listening intently to the B.B.C. news from London. His forbidden radio set was an old-fashioned one and the deprecating voice of the announcer sounded as if he were whispering in a mortuary.

"*. . . fifty-three enemy aircraft were destroyed. Nine of our aircraft failed to return but three of our pilots are safe. It is announced from Cairo that . . .*"

There was a sudden knock on the door. The Provost switched off the wireless, looked at his wife with raised eyebrows and nodded. As she left the parlour to open the door, the Provost concealed the receiving set under the Singer sewing machine cover. By the time his wife re-entered the room, followed by Captain Weiss, the Provost was sitting placidly in his armchair. He stood up, resting his gnarled hand on the wooden hood.

"Good evening, *Monsieur le Commandant.*"

"Good evening, *Monsieur le Provost.* I have permitted myself the pleasure of visiting you in your own home." He looked around him with interest, noting the pink paper fan, the fly-spotted oleograph, the plum plush and the aspidistra. It would be difficult to imagine a room so utterly representative of its owner and so transparently innocent. He said genially, "Well, what news?"

"News, monsieur? I . . . I do not understand. We have no news on the island other than what you tell us."

"Have no fears," he said soothingly. "From the German news bulletin you will learn nothing but the truth. I have some information for you. The island of Armorel has been selected as a training area for a special company of shock troops. They will carry out certain exercises in beach landings, cliff scaling and demolitions. They arrive to-morrow by the fast gunboat *Lübeck* and they will be quartered, for the few days that they are here, at the Abbaye itself. The gunboat will be in the *Havre des Mouettes*. The shock troops will be under independent command and, during their stay here, the most rigid security measures will be enforced. I regret that it will be necessary to extend the period of curfew. All islanders must remain in their homes between the hours of dusk and dawn. Those who disregard this order are likely to be fired on at sight."

"I will make the information known to the island, monsieur."

"Thank you. It is in the interests of the islanders themselves that this order is obeyed." The Provost walked with him into the hall, opened the door and accompanied him to the garden gate. For a full minute the two men stood in silence.

There was a host of stars in the sky and the soil of Armorel seemed to breathe the cool wet smell of autumn. Almost imperceptibly a sound slid into the quietness of the island night. It was an insistent, faraway droning that rose and fell with the wayward wind. The sound increased in volume. It became hard and constant and swelled into a snarl, into a hammering, into surges of thunder that rolled from the sky to the land so that the air itself seemed to quiver as squadron after squadron of German bombers flew blackly across the constant stars.

When the last of them had passed, when the sound of them was lost over the sea, silence fell like rain. Captain Weiss sighed.

"I am truly sorry," he said, "that England is so obstinate."

"I believe you, monsieur. And I believe that you will be sorrier still . . ."

Valentine Morland's voice stopped. Nicola said nothing. She was gazing at her empty coffee cup, her eyes absorbed.

She had listened to him without a word or a gesture, helping him not at all. Now the story was told. He had no knowledge whatsoever as to what strange thoughts lay behind the steadfast brightness of her eyes. It was a long time before she spoke. She looked at him, her head a little on one side.

"I'm afraid I'm not very good at history like you are. But there's one thing I do remember. It's rather apt, I think. In Ancient Rome, near the Capitol, there used to be a temple to Venus. It was set up because the Roman women, when their city was besieged by the Goths, cut off their hair to make bowstrings for their men. Do you think that's interesting?"

"Of course. But I don't see the connection."

"Don't you? Pity." She gave him a long, oblique glance. From the outskirts of London, the thin wail of an air-raid siren pierced the silence. The sound was taken up by a nearer siren—and by another and another, whooping and whining their urgent warning to the sullen city. Nicola's eyes widened. She said a little unsteadily:

"I've never heard that sound before. It's terrifying but timely. Here come the Goths." She paused, blinking. "It's not because of the air raid or the wine at dinner, but I think I'm going to cry a little. . . . Sorry."

CHAPTER TEN

GAY GO THE GORDONS . . .

DAWN came to London like a benediction and the melodious disharmony of the "All clear" sang its message of brief respite to an angry, weary people. Hermann Göring had been and gone, leaving several of his dark escort broken on the English fields. To-night he would come again. During the strenuous hours of daylight, London rolled up its sleeves to clear the streets, to heal the wounded and to bury the dead. Like the red corpuscles of the city's strong blood-stream, the defiant buses set out to crawl their deliberate way through the spew of bricks, past shattered houses from whose blind windows the smoke still curled sourly, and London took heart from their ponderous progress.

In the first light, a tall Highland sergeant walked the platform at King's Cross to the barrier. His rifle and steel helmet were slung on one shoulder and on the other he carried a packed kitbag. He walked with a slow, calm stride, his Gordon kilt swinging. He gave up his travel warrant, was passed through the barrier. A Military Police lance-corporal stepped forward.

"'Morning, Sergeant. Where are you for?"

"The War Office."

"Coo! Better the War Office than the war. Got your A.B. 64?"

"Aye. And here's the posting order."

The corporal read slowly. "3103210 Sgt. Alexander Forbes, Gordons, to report to Room 057 War Office 1000 hours. 15 September 1940." "O.K., Sergeant." He grinned and pointed to Alexander Forbes's rifle. "You won't want that when you get to the War Office. All you need there is a packet of paper-clips and a tea-cosy. You'll find the N.A.A.F.I. in the station yard. So long, Sarge."

"So long."

The corporal watched him go. He walked proudly, his back as straight as a lance. The corporal shook his head, turned to his companion.

"Imagine putting a bloke like that to lick bloody stamps in the War Office. No wonder old Hitler's got the laugh on us."

Trawler Langley opened one eye cautiously and immediately shut it again. For some minutes he lay perfectly still, his eyes tightly closed, while he attempted to put in some sort of order the kaleidoscopic events of last night. His thoughts came with difficulty because he had a splitting headache and a thirst that burned and raged like fire in the parched caverns of his gullet. He had been in the Strand when the sonorous voice of Big Ben had boomed the glad news that it was half-past five and therefore that the taverns of London were opening their hospitable doors. The first of them that he visited had been a clean, lonely shiny one, with chromium-plated chairs and a hoity-toity barmaid, who talked as if she had a plum in her mouth. It was not his sort of place so, after six bottles of Guinness, he had left, accidentally knocking over one of the chromium-plated chairs. He had picked it up and apologized like a gentleman, but the hoity-toity barmaid had merely given him a cool, contemptuous look and gone on polishing her nails. That was what had started it. Muttering, he had sallied out into the Strand and crossed the road to a more genial establishment where they sold Guinness out of the barrel. After three pints of draught and a large port, he had begged leave to tell the neutral barman exactly what he thought of Ireland in general and of Mr. de Valera in particular. When he had picked himself up and dusted his coat, he made his way purposefully to Covent Garden. By now his thirst was on him. He couldn't quite remember what had happened during the next hour or two. He had talked to some soldiers and he clearly remembered a Warrant Officer in the R.A.F., a man with a red face and some wings on his tunic that seemed to flap up and down. He had had a few straight gins with this one. But all the time he was thinking about the hoity-toity barmaid who hadn't even said "Granted, I'm sure" when he had done the decent thing and apologized like a gentleman for knocking over the chair. It wasn't right, that's what it wasn't. He had told the R.A.F. Warrant Officer with the red face and the flapping wings that it wasn't right and the Warrant Officer had agreed with him and said that if he were he, he'd have one more gin for the road and then one for swing of the door and then one for the gutter. After that he'd have one more for luck and then he'd go back to the posh pub with the hoity-toity barmaid and apologize again for knocking over the chair and see if she said "Granted, I'm sure" this time. "If she doesn't," said, the Warrant Officer with the utmost cordiality, "I'd break up the bloody place, I would. Cheerio, sailor, and down the hatch."

Down the hatch it was. There seemed to be a lot of noise about by now, guns going off and bombs dropping and fire-engines and ambulances clanging, and all the fun of the fair. Trawler Langley couldn't have cared less. He'd had one for the road, one for the swing of the door, and one for the gutter and a final double rum for luck. Then he had emerged into the cauldron of London, his hat on the back of his head, tears in his eyes and righteous indignation in his heart. . . .

A key rattled in the lock. Trawler sat up with a moan and opened his bloodshot eyes. A solemn policeman handed him a cup of scalding tea and, with infinite solicitude, two aspirins and a pocket comb. He said: "Bow Street 10 a.m. D. and D. Give me the comb back when you've done with it. It belongs to the missus."

Trawler Langley drank the tea, swallowed the aspirins and combed his hair and his beard. Then, somewhat shakily, he started on a tour of inspection of his cell. It was a lot better than some he'd been in in his time. . . .

Nicola Fallaize woke up in her aunt's flat in Sloane Street. She had not slept for long.

When the air raid had started, she, Valentine Morland and the *maître d'hôtel* of the Epicure had gone down to the wine cellar. There they had been joined by the Cypriot chef, the cashier and one of the waiters, who had crossed himself every time a bomb dropped. It had been a queer thing to sit among the wine bins calmly discussing the relative qualities of a Nuits St. Georges and a Pauillac while, over their heads, fire hoses played on burning houses and the Heavy Rescue Squads sought the dead amongst sliding, slanting girders. In a lull in the raid, Valentine had taken her home. They had walked the whole way and, sensing her fear, he had taken her arm and clasped her hand in his strong fingers. She had invited him to come in, for the cannonade had started again as they had reached her house, but he had refused. He had saluted her, standing on the step, and she had said, "Well, you might at least put your tin hat on," and he had said, "Frankly, I'd feel such an ass walking into Brown's in a tin hat," and she had said, "You'd feel even more of an ass if you were carried in," and he had said, "That's true. Look, may I call you Nicola? It seems silly not to," and she had said, "Of course you must call me Nicola. Obviously. And thank you so much for dinner."

She began to think about Valentine, this man into whose company she had been flung only a few hours ago. The fact that she had danced with him in Oxford two years ago didn't count, for he hadn't even seen her then. But he had seen her now. She was acutely aware that he had seen her . . . and that the Oxford frock had been avenged. She had always held herself aloof from the easy intimacies that were apt to ripen so readily in the forcing house of war. This was no slick subaltern who regarded all passable women in uniform as fair game and all staff cars as mobile *boîtes d'amour*; this was no amorous Colonel with a wife and five children conveniently tucked away in North Cornwall. This was a man who might well interest any woman deeply, even dangerously, for he was strong and kind and considerate and he had a most disarming preoccupation with a cause. He had told her of the Venus project simply and without embellishment and she had listened in mounting delight, well content to know that the age of chivalry was not past. In the silence that followed he had said almost apologetically: "The whole thing may sound ridiculous to you. But it isn't a cow in calf at all. It's the preservation of a dynasty."

"You don't need to tell me that. My father bred Venus."

She was young and healthy and solitary in England. It would be very easy to become interested in a man who, by some subtle alchemy, made her feel that she was indeed what he had called her—a Princess. It *would* be easy . . . if she were as other women. But she wasn't. She was bound forever to a man who walked in freedom the very soil which could readily become Valentine Morland's grave.

"Nicola, something awful's happened. Some extraordinary man calling himself Uncle George has just telephoned from the War Office and they're sending round a car for you in a quarter of an hour. What do you think it is?"

Nicola jumped out of bed.

"After yesterday, anything can happen. I expect they're sending me by submarine to Tokio. Aunt Heloise, can you lend me some Silvo and a button-stick—and a Japanese phrase book?"

"Darling, you can't go to Tokio without any breakfast. Really, I do think the War Office is most inconsiderate. . . ."

Nicola walked into Room 057, saluted. The Brigadier was listening to the eight-o'clock news on a portable set. He switched it off as she entered and stood up.

"Good morning, Miss Fallaize."

"Good morning, sir."

"Please don't call me 'sir'. My name is Uncle George. Have you had breakfast?"

"No. I've had a cup of tea."

"Have some more. It's beastly tea, but do have some." He picked up the receiver and ordered a pot of tea for two to be sent down from the canteen. He said, "Do you smoke?"

"Not at this time of the morning," she said faintly.

He smiled. "Yes, it is a little early. I'm sorry to bring you out at cock-crow, but I want to talk to you privately—before you see Major Morland again. When

I say privately I mean privately. That goes for everybody—including Major Morland. You understand?"

"I do."

"When are you meeting Valentine again?"

"He's coming to pick me up at my aunt's house at half-past nine."

"That gives us over an hour." He looked at her shrewdly. "Tell me, what do you think of Operation Venus?"

So this was it! She looked at him, her face politely mystified.

"Operation Venus? I'm afraid I don't know what you mean."

There was a knock on the door and a waitress came in with two cups of tea on a tray. She said in a dispirited voice, "That'll be fourpence, sir," and Uncle George put the money on the tray. She trailed out disconsolately.

"So you don't know anything about Operation Venus?"

Nicola shook her head. "It sounds vaguely astronomical. Do tell me about it."

"Would you recognize Valentine's voice?"

"I think so. Yes, I'm sure I would."

He picked up the telephone again and said, "Get me Major Morland at Brown's Hotel, please." He put down the receiver and pointed. "When he comes through, will you listen in on that extension."

"Certainly, sir."

"I asked you not to call me 'sir'. Have some tea before a film of ice forms over it."

Uncle George looked at her from under bushy eyebrows. Every word that she had said—or had not said—had served to confirm and to strengthen his half-formed plan. When the telephone bell rang, he waved her towards the extension line. She picked it up and listened.

"Valentine?"

"Yes. 'Morning, Uncle George."

"I told you yesterday that you were free to discuss a certain project with Miss Fallaize. Did you do so?"

"I did."

"So there's nothing about Operation Venus that she doesn't know?"

"Nothing. Why, Uncle George? She's absolutely reliable. Absolutely."

"I am increasingly aware of it. Come in and see me when you've pulled your bearded boy friend out of Bow Street. Good-bye."

Nicola and Uncle George put down their two telephones simultaneously. He smiled at her. She smiled back. He said genially:

"Well, my security-minded cook-cowherd, are you ready to talk about Operation Venus now?"

"Certainly, Uncle George."

The magistrate gazed at Trawler Langley over his spectacles.

"You appear to be a sea-faring man."

Trawler shuffled his feet.

"Yes, sir . . . Your Worship."

"It is, to my mind, a lamentable thing that no suitable employment can be found for a person such as you in times like these. Instead of roistering in the Strand," he said sternly, "you should be serving your country. What is your age?"

"Thirty-seven, Your Worship . . . sir."

"The accused is sixty-one, Your Worship," said the policeman gently.

"Oh. That puts a different complexion on it. You will pay a fine of five shillings. Next case, please."

Trawler Langley paid two morose half-crowns to the jailer and walked out into the freedom of Bow Street. What he wanted more than anything on the face of the earth was a nice cold bottle of Bass. . . .

"Mr. Langley."

Trawler swung round defensively. A military officer in uniform was looking at him with a smile that was wholly sympathetic.

"Yes. I'm Langley."

"My name is Morland. I think that you and this lady have met before."

From behind the military officer a young woman stepped forward and held out her hand. She said, "Hullo, Trawler."

He stared at her, his eyes wide. Then he gave a great, free shout that sent the pigeons of Bow Street wheeling and circling over the roofs.

"Miss Nicola, by God! Do I know Miss Nicola? I helped her cousin to pull a mackerel hook out of her behind when she was six."

"I hope it didn't leave a mark," said Valentine. "Come and have a drink."

Trawler Langley sat in a pub in Maiden Lane, a bottle of Bass at his elbow, a pipe in his mouth and joy in his heart. He had talked to Miss Nicola without ceasing, gushing with reminiscence of the islands, and now, at last, a long silence had fallen between them. The military officer, Major Morland or something, leaned forward. He said quietly:

"How would you like to go to sea again, Langley? Back to the islands . . ."

"How would I like to go to sea. . . ."

It seemed to him that he couldn't have heard aright. He said again huskily, "How would I like to go to sea. . . ." He stared at the officer. Then he looked at Miss Nicola. He looked back at the officer. His eyes seemed to find difficulty in focusing for the officer's face dissolved and swam and he was aware, with gulping shame, that tears were flowing and crawling down his cheeks to lose themselves in the tangle of his beard. When he could trust himself to speak he said gruffly:

"I'd like that very much, sir."

In a quiet corner of the War Office library, Valentine Morland folded up a map of Armorel and gave it to Alexander Forbes.

"Well, there you are, Alec. Study it till you know that island like the inside of your hand and keep it locked up. I've arranged for you to see the Signals boys at four and you'll fix your transmission set and schedule with them. Now are there any questions?"

Sergeant Forbes thought very carefully. A full minute passed before he answered.

"No, Mr. Valentine. No questions." He chuckled. "This is better than the first day we saw the redshank in the nest and that was a grand day. I've always wanted to visit Armorel for the cliffs are haunted by birds. There are cormorants and puffins and the Greater Black-backed Gull——"

"What I want you to concentrate on is the Greater Red-backed Cow. See you to-morrow, Alec, in Room 057, at 10 o'clock."

"Right, Mr. Valentine." He drew himself up to attention, smiled his slow smile and left the library. Valentine turned to Trawler Langley.

"Well, you know what your job is. You help to pilot us in, do a recce on the spot and return to England. Then the next night, you collect us by M.T.B. A craft is being specially fitted out for the job. The lower deck has been stripped, the torpedo tubes removed and a hatchway made. She is being fitted with special hoisting gear. Combined Ops. will go into all that with you and also work out your timing. The first thing for you to do is to get down to Oxford for general briefing and then you can work out details with Combined Ops. to-morrow. When you get to Oxford, keep out of the pubs." He laughed. "No roistering in the High, in fact. Anything you're not sure about?"

"Yes, sir, there is. Suppose when we come to Armorel to pick you up, you're not there waiting. What happens then?"

"If we're not there on time, it means that Operation Venus has failed. Your orders then are to turn and go licketty split for home."

"Leaving you and Sergeant Forbes on the island."

"Exactly. Leaving Sergeant Forbes and me to . . . to . . . well, find our own way home."

Trawler Langley grinned and jutted out his beard.

"I hear what you say, Major Morland."

"And you'll do what I say, Langley," he replied evenly. "Now you'd better collect a warrant and catch the 4.45 from Paddington to Oxford. They've been warned that you're coming and they've got a jug of tomato juice on the ice. See you to-morrow."

"Aye, aye, sir."

When he had gone, Valentine looked with sudden startled recognition at Nicola. It seemed to him at that moment that he had known her all his life. There was a quite extraordinary sense of familiarity, almost of intimacy between them, and it was with a feeling of wonder that he realized that they had met a mere twenty-four hours ago. He said to her, speaking slowly:

"It's absurd. I feel as if I'd known you for a very long time."

She was afraid to answer him as she wanted to, afraid to speak freely, afraid to say that she too completely shared the sense of long comradeship. Instead of uttering the revealing words that sprang to the root of her tongue, she shrugged. She said lightly:

"Possibly in a previous incarnation, we knew each other quite well. I may have been Cleopatra and you . . . and you . . ." She faltered and stopped. "What I mean is, you may have been Saint Benedict and I his nurse. You may even have been Solomon and I a harem lady. Sorry. I am being silly. I don't know what I mean. . . ." She went on quickly, very much on the defensive. "I like your Alexander Forbes very much. All that slow, calm majesty—and a Gordon kilt as well."

"What may I bring you back from Armorel, Nicola?"

She glanced at him quickly. This was the opening she had waited for ever since her astonishing meeting with Uncle George that morning. He had insisted that she should break the ice with Valentine, knowing full well what his immediate and wholly characteristic reaction would be. She looked carefully at an old coloured print on the wall. It was a print of a Rifleman in the 60th, a spidery, long-moustached gentleman who leaned on a musket. She wondered, with an inward giggle, what he would have said if Her Gracious Majesty, Queen Victoria, had suggested that it was within his military duty to set sail for the Channel Islands and kidnap a nineteenth-century cow.

"What do I want you to bring me back? I want you to bring us all back, Alexander Forbes, Trawler, you, me—plus Venus. That's what I want most of all."

"But you're not coming," he said steadily. "You are not coming, Nicola."

"May I have a cigarette?" she asked.

"Certainly." He lit it for her. She began to speak, aware of his hostility, choosing her words with care.

"When you asked me about Armorel, I told you a lot of things. I told you the ordinary, superficial things because I didn't know anything about Operation Venus then. Now I do know. I'm not a conceited person. I'm a very humble, frightened one, but I do know one thing. Unless you take me with you, Operation Venus will fail, and you and Alec will end the war either in a prison camp or six feet down in the soil of Armorel. And I wouldn't like that at all."

"Why should Operation Venus fail?"

"Because you don't know the island and the island doesn't know you. The islanders are enclosed now and they would be deeply suspicious of you. They wouldn't know who you were and they wouldn't trust you. Nobody would give you away. That is quite sure. But if you are going to get Venus away, you need help. It sounds silly, but you need the people and the soil on your side. Armorel is not a country. It is a community. Let me give you one example. You don't know at what points on the cliffs the German sentries are posted."

"Do you?" He smiled.

"No. But the moment we land, I can go to any one of my three hundred friends and find out. So could my brother Luke if he were here. You can't because no one would tell you. Luke isn't here, but I am."

She paused. "You call me Nicola. May I call you Valentine?"

"Of course. I thought you did."

"No. I've studiously called you nothing. Please tell me, why don't you want me to come?"

"Why don't I want you to come?" He hesitated. "You said a moment ago that Alec and I might end the war either in the can or . . . elsewhere. I should think that that's roughly true. If you were a man, if you were your brother Luke, it would be different."

"How so?" she said with interest.

"Well, you're made the wrong shape, that's all."

"Shapes don't matter in wartime."

"Don't they?"

She looked away. The ice that had filmed his voice was melting, melting and flowing. For the first time in her life, she was glad that she was wearing uniform and even more glad that he had seen her last night when she wasn't. She said meekly:

"I'd be a lot safer in Armorel than in the blitz. London is a lot more dangerous than Armorel. Specially," she added, "when I have to drive majors about who sit in the front seat."

He said to her very solemnly:

"Do you want to come?"

Her mood reflected his mood. She said:

"I want to come because I know that I can be useful to you. I said once to somebody, to my cousin Lionel actually, that I was a woman and that, because of that, I couldn't do much in a war. This is a moment when

I can do something—in spite of my regrettable shape. But if you ask me if I, Nicola, want to go back to Armorel, the answer is 'no, I don't'."

"Why?"

She looked him full in the face. He was a fine, clean man and she liked him deeply.

"How would you care," she said, "to go back to a haunted house?"

CHAPTER ELEVEN

HAND OF STEEL

It was mid-afternoon when a curious little party of four crossed the deck of a depot ship in Portsmouth, descended to the outer casing of a submarine and climbed up the conning-tower ladder to the bridge. There the Captain awaited them. He was a young, bearded Lieutenant R.N. and he gazed with an amateur's envy at the luxuriant whiskers worn by one of the party. He led them down through the conning-tower hatch to the control room, held back a curtain at the forward end and they passed into a tiny, lit wardroom. There he surveyed his passengers.

Nicola wore a grey-blue Shetland sweater and a much mended Harris tweed skirt. The Captain looked at her, frowning, then shrugged slightly. It was, he supposed, no business of his and presumably the War Office knew what they were up to. Valentine Morland, obviously the leader of the party, was in dirty flannel trousers and a navy blue jersey. He had a tightly packed haversack slung on one shoulder and a Colt automatic at his hip. Alexander Forbes, in an equally anonymous blue jersey, carried a cheap fibre suitcase and a coil of rope round his waist. The Captain, unaware that a B.2 transmitting and receiving set had been skilfully built into the suitcase, wondered why this tall Pongo with the blue eyes should want to take his pyjamas and sponge bag with him. Then he looked at Trawler Langley and absently fingered his short beard. It would take him months to grow one to equal that bushy magnificence. Trawler was in a patched Merchant Navy uniform and peaked cap to which he had characteristically added the skull and crossbones badge of the 17th Lancers.

Quietly, almost lazily, the Captain explained the procedure. He might as easily have been describing the workings of Boulter's Lock on a sunny peace-time afternoon to an excursion party.

"We shall be shoving off almost at once and I expect we'll have a quiet trip. That of course depends on our little airborne friends of the Luftwaffe. We'll stay on the surface as long as we can because there are some complicated and tiresome minefields about and navigation under water through minefields is rather a bore. If our little friends do show up, we'll have to dive—quite quickly actually. Bells ring and hooters hoot and that sort of thing and that's how you know. You'll find it quite comfortable down here, if a little stuffy after a bit. We hope to put you ashore at a place called Petit Pigeon Bay. Then we'll submerge again and push off to a point thirty-five cables west of the point and lie doggo for exactly thirty minutes when we'll surface and pick up the gentleman in the beautiful beard and beat it for England, home and beauty. All clear?"

"All clear."

"There are biscuits and cocoa in the galley and drinks in the locker." He looked at Nicola. He said slowly, speaking with embarrassment, "I was unaware until this moment that one of my passengers was to be a woman. All I can say is that my hat is off to you, madam."

He turned abruptly and went into the control room.

Nicola sat down. She was completely calm, completely absorbed by all about her. Trawler prowled round the wardroom, opened a locker and produced a bottle of Plymouth gin and four glasses with a triumphant chuckle. Valentine said quickly:

"Save that up for the return trip, Trawler."

"It's good for sea-sickness, Skipper."

"I've got some pills for that, Trawler. Put it back."

"O.K., Skipper. You win."

He put back the bottle. Alexander Forbes slid his hand into his pocket, produced a half-tied trout fly and began to manipulate the delicate feather with expert, loving fingers. Valentine spread a crumpled map of Armorel on the wardroom table. As he began to speak, there was a slight jerk followed immediately by the steady rumble of Diesel engines. Valentine stopped in mid-sentence. Neither he nor Nicola spoke, because there was nothing to say.

Almost imperceptibly the submarine slid away from the depot ship and moved forward to slice the smooth waters of the harbour into rippling waves. On the bridge, the Captain gave curt orders into his speaking tube and two duffle-coated ratings scanned the dusk unceasingly as the submarine lifted her bows to the first surges of the open sea.

From the dark and menaced shore of England she looked like a long diminishing shadow on the sea. She became smaller and smaller till, suddenly, she merged into the sea itself. Over the empty space of water where she had set out on her perilous journey the words of Winston Churchill followed in the hidden bubbles of her wake:

"There comes from the sea a hand of steel which plucks the German sentries from their posts. . . ."

In the little wardroom of the submerged submarine, Valentine Morland glanced at Alexander Forbes. His voice was steady in the almost uncanny silence.

"Well, Alec, do you think you could find your way round Armorel?"

Alec spoke with the quiet confidence of one who had spent his life in lonely places.

"Provided the map's accurate, yes."

"You, Langley?"

Trawler Langley laughed shortly. "I don't know the land but, by God, I know the sea."

"That's all we ask of you, that you should know the sea. You know your timings?"

"I do."

"What are they?"

"You, Miss Nicola, Forbes and the cow will be at the *Pointe de Joie* at high water, which is 1016 G.M.T., waiting to be taken off." He ran his fingers through his beard. "For God's sake don't be late. The tide goes out at the *Pointe de Joie* like a dose of salts and there will only be enough water for half an hour at most. Suppose the weather breaks . . . I know the *Pointe de Joie* in a north-easter and it isn't funny."

"We won't be late."

Alexander Forbes's fingers were still busy with his trout fly. But his mind was far away in the wind-blown Hebrides. He was thinking with delight of an evening long ago when he and Mr. Valentine had been coming home at the time of the declining of the sun. They had heard a sound that was not of this world and, looking up, they had seen a long, wavering line etched against the illimitable distances of the sky and they had watched that etched line move from the steeps to the steeps as the wild geese flew in a sweet arrowhead across the strengthening stars.

"Stand by to surface."

There was a sudden gushing sound of water bubbling, and the Captain was up the ladder like a cat. He was followed by another officer and two ratings. A draught of cool air came into the submarine like a benediction.

Valentine said to Nicola: "This is it."

"Yes. This is it."

She climbed the ladder of the conning-tower hatch on to the bridge and looked around her. The night was dark and there was a vast silence. As her eyes became accustomed to the darkness, she saw a greater darkness looming to starboard and she knew with fear and with joy that she was gazing on the cliffs of her home.

CHAPTER TWELVE

JEWELLED HILT

In the sea-murmurous quietness, Valentine could hear the soft, rhythmic splash of paddles as Trawler wavered his rubber dinghy out to his submarine rendezvous. Soon that little sound was lost in the incessant surge and ebb of the long-backed breakers. The moon was in the second quarter and the tall shadow of Alexander Forbes slanted blue-black in the tide-washed stones. A seabird called sleepily from the distant cliff and was silent again. Valentine half-turned to Nicola. He said in a whisper:

"Now we really are committed."

"We always were."

He sensed her tension. "Nervous?"

She shook her head in the gloom. "Much worse than that. I'm scared stiff." There was a moment's silence. "But I wouldn't change places with anyone in the world."

"Neither would I. Give me your hand, Nicola."

He took her hand in his. Her fingers were as cold as ice and he could feel a constant quiver in her muscles. For a long time he held her hand, standing perfectly still, trying with all his will-power to calm her with his strength. Under the firm pressure of his hand, the fluttering became intermittent, died away. Only when her fingers, her knees and her breathing were steady did she clasp his hand briefly and strongly and draw away.

"Sorry I was such a fool. I'm fine now. What's the next move?"

"You guide us up the cliff and inland. We haven't been spotted—yet. But there may be a sentry on the cliff-head so don't make a sound as we go up."

"I won't. If there is a sentry there, what happens?"

"Alec and I will cope with him. Don't worry. You know what to do, Alec?"

Alexander Forbes smiled. He twisted something that trailed in his fingers. "I do, Mr. Valentine."

"Right. Off we go."

The three moved into the half-darkness, Nicola leading. The path up the cliff was sloping and stony and once Valentine's nailed shoe scraped against an outspur of rock. In the stillness a dog barked furiously, senselessly, a long way away and they listened, motionless as statues. A light wind moved the bracken and rustled drily in the reeds of a pool that glimmered in a hollow of the hill. Nicola said in a whisper:

"That's Tadpole Pond. I used to collect frog-spawn there when I was little. But it never turned into frogs."

Alec whispered very seriously:

"I don't suppose you kept it at the right temperature. Frog-spawn's fickle." He had two feet of thin rope in his fingers with a loop and a slip knot. He flexed his muscular fingers.

"You must tell me about frog-spawn when we get back, Alec."

"I will."

She was cool and excited now, with every nerve as taut as an E string. She moved on and the two men followed on tiptoe. In a few minutes they reached the top of the cliff where the path flattened out into a track that skirted a field of stubble. Carefully Nicola looked around her. This, she knew, was the first high point of danger and it was with a great sigh of relief that she saw the long empty levels of the mown wheat. She whispered, breathing deeply:

"Not a soul in sight. The luck's with us still. We take this track and cross the Sevriers' farm."

It was difficult to follow, for she moved as silently as a ghost. Alexander Forbes philosophically slid the length of rope into his pocket. This was only the start of this adventure and it might well be that he would use it yet. Keeping well in the shadow of the hedge, they reached the open gate to the Sevriers' farm. As they crossed the puddled yard, Nicola glanced up at the heavily curtained windows. Did she imagine it—or was it true that she saw a tiny, momentary splinter of candle-light as a curtain was stealthily slid to one side, allowed to fall back again? She narrowed her eyes. Pierre and Juliette Sevrier would long ago have been in bed and asleep but the whereabouts of their nephew, Georges, was a different matter. She thought of Georges with affection. The Provost's grandson was a thin, self-possessed little boy of about ten, an expert poacher, shrimp-fisher and parsnip thief, and she had often speculated upon how the somewhat pedestrian German mind would react to his innocence and his guile. Anyway, from Georges she knew that she had nothing to fear. *En avant!*

Now they took to the field. There was something almost ominous in the silence that encompassed the island and strange it was indeed to realize that the air they breathed was also being drawn into enemy lungs. Valentine and Alec followed her quietly, unquestioning, and she was warmed by the knowledge of their absolute confidence in her, their sure-footed guide. Soon she came to a low stone wall and climbed it. Beyond was a patch of deep gorse and in its shadow she stopped. She pointed to a dark shape that loomed on the crest of the hill over a dim, moonlit valley.

"That's the Abbaye."

They all three peered across the night. Valentine whispered, "And to the left of it is what might be called the Temple of Venus."

"Exactly."

"And we've got to cross a road to get there."

"Yes. We can't avoid the road. Not by any means."

"Then there's only one way to do it. Let's sit down and rest for a minute while I explain."

They sat down on the cool ground. Valentine said what he proposed to do and why and they agreed with him, discussing it calmly, accepting its danger without comment. Soon they spoke no more. The wind was gentle and Nicola leaned back on her elbows and gazed up into the illimitable distances of the sky. Within the moon's bright orbit the stars were pale, but she gazed on the mighty radiance of the Milky Way and on the jewelled hilt of Orion's Sword. How limpid the night, how strong the surges of blood from her heart, how joyous to be home. She slid her hand along the grass so that the blades came between her fingers and she held them firmly, caressing the earth beneath with her finger-tips. She knew that life could hold no moment comparable to this, and that the years that she had lived before were like hollow, dusty rooms. "It is better to remain unborn," said a Greek philosopher two thousand years ago, but she rejoiced to know that he lied. At some hour she would die. But if inevitable death were to quicken his pace and take her now, she would go gladly in this place and in the good company of these men. A star detached itself from a star and fled, shining, down the sky and a hand that was not her hand touched her shoulder.

"Nicola . . . did you see that?"

"Yes, I saw it."

"And did you wish?"

"Of course. Did you?"

"Naturally."

She sat up on one elbow. "You mustn't tell me what your wish is," she said solemnly, "or it may not come true."

"I know that." He stood up as soundlessly as a leopard. "This is the moment to go on."

"Of course it is. We're safe now—anyway until the dawn. We have been blessed by a star."

They crossed the long slope of the valley, moving stealthily in the shadow of the gorse. At the summit of the incline they came to the edge of the road that led past the Abbaye. Here they stopped. Valentine said easily:

"Now for it. You come between us, Nicola. Alec, you'll have to shorten that long Highland stride of yours. All ready?"

"All ready."

"Good." He chuckled. "By the left—quick march."

As if led by the massed drums and pipes of the Gordons, they wheeled on to the road and marched abreast towards the Abbaye, their heads up and their heels ringing in the silence of the night. They passed a shuttered cottage, crossed a pool of darkness cast by two tall trees and swung round a bend. The old walls of the Abbaye loomed jet-black in the moonlight . . . and the spectral drums beat to a crescendo of thunder, drowning the scream of the pipes and the crunch of their marching feet. . . . Sixty yards to go, forty, thirty . . . twenty . . .

At the gate of the Abbaye, the German sentry heard their martial approach and peered frowning into the gloom. The special shock troops who had arrived on the island were out at all hours of the night. They were tough, hard-eyed and silent and they did not take kindly to questions. Dimly he saw them coming, two tall shapes and a shorter one between them. He stiffened to attention and stared woodenly to his front. As the little rank of three passed him, one of them gave him a guttural "*Gute Nacht und Heil Hitler!*" and he rapped out his ludicrous stereotyped reply, "*Heil Hitler!*" It was rare indeed that these demi-gods even had the courtesy to acknowledge the presence of the garrison and the sentry relaxed with a grin. That desirable closer liaison between varying arms of the Wehrmacht was obviously improving! He heard rather than saw them turn to the left towards the stables, heard the sound of their marching footsteps become faint in the night, stop. His had been an uneventful two hours and there was still nothing to report. He yawned and went back to thinking with longing of his Gertrude in Poppenbüttel. . . .

Nicola said suddenly, "Here we are."

There was a huge water-butt by the door to a small, square building. She pressed the latch with a little click and the half-door swung open. She put her arm inside, felt for the bolt, drew it back. The bottom half opened with a strident, rusty whine that set her heart racing. She slipped into the stable with Valentine and Alec at her heels. It was pitch dark and she shut the door slowly and with infinite care.

"Next time I'll bring an oil-can," she whispered. "I should have remembered that rusty hinge. Valentine, when you said '*Heil Hitler!*' my knees turned to water. Give me your torch." The darkness was opaque and seemed to press on her lids. She found his hand and took the torch from him and drew him after her. She said almost soundlessly in his ear:

"Are you ready?"

"Yes."

A bright pencil of light sprang on to the floor, travelled away, slanted slightly upwards. In its beam, a sleepy cow turned her head lazily, blinking her soft, fringed eyes. She was contentedly chewing the cud and Valentine saw that her belly was full and her udder low down. For a long time he and Alec gazed at her. Then the light flicked off. He heard Nicola's soothing, excited whisper in the scented darkness:

"Hullo, Venus. We've come to take you home."

CHAPTER THIRTEEN

DANS LE JARDIN DE MON PÈRE

DAWN rose over the sea and the sun leapt in light up the dark cliffs of Armorel. A German soldier marched to the gate of the hotel where the garrison was quartered, wiped his mouth and raised a bugle to his lips. The brazen melody romped over the autumnal fields and echoed thinly among the high thorn bushes, bright with drops of dew. The Provost, early astir, heard the sound and sighed, unaware that the tumbling notes were calling him to a true reveille. Lionel Fallaize stretched in his sleep and muttered and sank back into a dream-haunted coma of light and half-light and curious shapes. The islanders of Armorel opened their doors after the night and breathed the morning air, free for a few brief hours to walk their own soil.

One dusty sunbeam shone through the cob-webbed window of the hay-loft over the stable where Venus ruminated contentedly in her stall. It rested momentarily on a black and white tom cat busily washing his face and moved on to illuminate a girl's ankles, motionless in sleep. As the bugle's call pierced the morning, the ankles jerked into wakefulness and Nicola sat up with a start, wide-eyed. She looked around her, shook her head and drew a long, quivering breath.

"So it's true. We are here."

"Yes. It's true. Good morning, Nicola."

"Good morning, Valentine. Hullo, Alec."

"Hullo, Miss Nicola. How did you sleep?"

"Very well, I think. I'm not sure." The tom cat, its toilet completed, was watching her with interest. She stretched out her hand and called it. It came over to her and rubbed itself against her fingers, purring and arching its back. She said, scratching its head, "This is Dum. He had a sister called Dee but we had to put Dee down. I didn't think cats remembered people."

"Dum certainly remembers you. Have a sandwich."

"I'm not terribly hungry. Give me a bit of yours."

She brushed a few wisps of hay off her shoulders. The loft was dim in the corners but motes danced in the shaft of sunshine that filtered through the cobwebs. Alexander Forbes glanced at his watch and touched Valentine on the shoulder. He said, "Three minutes to go."

"What are you going to do, Alec?" she asked with interest.

"Transmit to London. We fixed the aerial while you were asleep."

The fibre suitcase was open and Nicola looked with curiosity at the complicated mechanism of the B.2 set with its earphones and Morse tapper. Valentine and Alec were gazing at the second-hands of their respective watches. Valentine said in a low voice: "We'll do it in clear. There are no radio detection cars in Armorel—yet! Ready, Alec?"

Alec adjusted his earphones and sent out his call sign,

listened frowning for the "am receiving you loud and clear, loud and clear", jerked up his thumb. Very slowly Valentine began to dictate:

FOR UNCLE GEORGE FROM VALENTINE STOP HAVE CONTACTED VENUS WHO IS IN THE ASCENDANT . . .

He stopped, suddenly alert. Slow footsteps sounded on the road outside and the stable door opened with its rusty whine. Lying flat in the hay, Nicola peered over the edge of the loft. Below her was Baptiste. As he walked ponderously over to Venus, she got up and stretched. Baptiste ran his hand along her back and began talking to her in Armorel patois, making meaningless, affectionate sounds with his mouth. He took an armful of maize from the back of the stable and gave it to her and she began to eat. Baptiste started to do the simple tasks he had done for fifty years. He turned over her bedding of bracken with a dung fork, spreading it evenly. Then he took a long-handled brush and swept out the manure gutter, hissing softly between his teeth as he worked. Nicola looked at Valentine and smiled like an excited schoolgirl. She said softly, "It's Baptiste. I have known him all my life. It's quite safe. You can carry on." She stood up and walked very quietly down the wooden stairs into the sunny stable.

"*Bonjour, Baptiste.*"

The old man looked up from his sweeping. He gazed at her with his clear blue eyes and a look of utter amazement spread over his face.

"*C'est . . . c'est vous. C'est Mademoiselle Nicola.*"

"*Oui, Baptiste. C'est moi.*"

"*Mais . . . mais qu'est-ce que vous faites ici en Armorel, Mademoiselle?*"

"*Ecoutez, Baptiste*——"

She walked over to him and took his old gnarled hand in hers. Up in the hay-loft, Valentine and Alec could hear the murmur of their voices. As Valentine went on with his whispered dictation, the Morse tapper took up its soft staccato stammer:

PLEASE CONTINUE TO STAND BY STOP LOCAL INFORMATION COMING UP IMMEDIATELY——

He looked up. New steps sounded on the road. They were firm, decisive steps and they approached the stable purposefully. Nicola was up the wooden stairs like a flash and had just managed to reach the loft when the stable door opened. Alec's fingers froze into immobility over his Morse tapper. The door swung back with that ominous whine that they were beginning to know so well and a man's booted feet crossed the stable towards Venus's stall. A voice spoke in good guttural English: "Good morning, Baptiste."

There was a long pause. Baptiste said huskily:

"Good morning, *Monsieur le Commandant*."

In the hay-loft the three scarcely dared to breathe. They heard leisurely steps in the manure gutter as Captain Weiss viewed Venus from every side. He began to speak, affectionately stroking her quarters.

"And how is my darling this morning, *mein Liebchen*?" He stepped back. "She looks very well, Baptiste, and I think she will bear her calf very soon. Perhaps to-day or to-morrow. Surely this week. I am quite sure that it will be a bull." He glanced round at Baptiste and frowned. "What is the matter with you? You look like Mr. Lionel Fallaize—as if you have seen a ghost."

"I have seen nothing, monsieur. Nothing . . ."

"Too much brandy last night, eh, Baptiste? You will not take Venus out until the dew is off the grass and then you will peg her down in the top pasture. She is always a joy for me to see." He gave Venus a last, gentle slap. "Soon you will eat the richer grass of Westphalia, you and your noble son."

Nicola's right foot was doubled up underneath her in the hay and the ache was becoming unbearable. She clenched her teeth as a sword of pain slid agonizingly along her muscle. With infinite care she freed her foot, stretched it out silently. It encountered an obstruction and she pressed strongly. To her horror the obstruction moved . . . and a turnip as big as a football rolled drunkenly across the uneven boards. With all the calculated malice of an inanimate object, the turnip came to a stop at the head of the wooden stairs, rocked for a breathless moment between two boards, turned slowly round and fell bumping and crashing from step to step on to the stable floor.

Captain Weiss swung round, his hand leaping to the butt of his automatic. He drew his pistol and cocked it, staring narrow-eyed at the edge of the loft. He took a stride forward—and suddenly stopped with a chuckle. Walking on delicate paws, a black and white tom cat stepped leisurely down from the loft, sat down on the stairs for a moment to scratch its ear, yawned and walked with infinite dignity into the sunshine.

Captain Weiss's chuckle became a laugh. He thrust his pistol back into its holster and walked to the door. He turned round for a last look at Venus. He was in high good humour and he saluted her bony rump.

"*Auf wiedersehen, mein Liebchen.*"

When the door had shut behind him, when the sound of his steps was lost in the mounting bustle of the morning, Valentine wiped the sweat off his forehead. He glanced at Alec who smiled his slow smile and with rare tact neither of them looked at Nicola. Valentine resumed his slow dictation:

REGRET UNAVOIDABLE INTERRUPTIONS STOP HAVE OVERHEARD COMMANDANT'S PLAN TO INVEIGLE PRIMA DONNA TO REICH STOP WILL DO ALL POSSIBLE TO FRUSTRATE STOP PLEASE CONTRIBUTE FIVE REPEAT FIVE POUNDS TO LOCAL CATS HOME STOP ENDS.

When Alec had finished his message, he packed his earphones and Morse tapper into the fibre suitcase and shut it. Valentine pulled out his inevitable map.

"Now this is the form. You, Nicola, will make your way to the Provost through the gardens and the orchard. How long do you think you'll be with him?"

"Half an hour, three-quarters. It depends. I've got a lot to find out."

"Call it an hour. Alec and I will leave here separately and make different circuits ending up at this point." He put his finger on a small, sheltered copse. "You will meet us there in sixty minutes exactly with as much information as you've got. In the light of what you tell us, we'll decide on how to organize the job in detail. All clear?"

"All clear."

"Good. We'll now synchronize our watches and you can start." She stood up. He said with studied unconcern: "There's only one more thing. If one of us has the bad luck to run into trouble, the other two carry on—no matter what happens to the unlucky one. Is that quite clearly understood?"

After a moment's pause, Nicola said in a low voice: "Yes. That's understood. Don't eat all the sandwiches. *Au revoir, chers amis.*"

She climbed down the ladder into the stable, patted Venus affectionately on the flank, and slipped out into the morning.

The Provost of Armorel, collarless, the laces of his boots trailing and yesterday's stubble still grey on his jowl, went out through the kitchen door with a basin of oats to feed the hens. He called them to him with soft, clucking noises and they came running and fluttering to pick and to squabble and squawk over the yellow grain. When the last handful had been flung, he searched the rickety hen-house for eggs, knowing exactly where to look. There were three brown ones in the nests and—as usual—another behind the old rusty sundial in the corner. He put the four eggs in the basin and began to sweep. He heard his wife calling. There was a note of urgency, a note almost of fear in her voice and he went quickly to the door of the hen-house. He shouted over the little garden:

"What is it, Marie?"

"Come. Come." She beckoned to him. "Come at once. Come now, immediately."

He walked back through the garden to the kitchen door. Marie stood there. He saw that her face was white and that she breathed in gasps. She caught his arm with trembling fingers. For a moment she was unable to speak. He said, "What is it? Are you ill? Tell me, Marie."

"*Mon Dieu*, I am not ill but ashamed. You are dirty and you have not shaved. Where is your collar, your tie? Look at your boots—and you the Provost of Armorel. Oh my God . . ."

"But, Marie . . ."

"Go quickly into the bedroom and shave. Quickly. Put on your good suit and, for the love of God, your collar and tie. I will polish your boots. Give them to me. Jacques, be quick."

He shouted at her, his mouth working:

"I demand that you tell me. What has happened?"

"What has happened?" She drew a long, shuddering breath. "I will tell you what has happened. You are the Provost of Armorel and it is thus that you wish to greet the sister of our Suzerain."

"What do you mean? Woman, what do you mean?"

"I mean," she said, sobbing without restraint, "that Miss Nicola has come back to us. She is in this house. Almighty God has sent Miss Nicola back to us. . . ."

There was a warm glow in the heart of the September sun now, a glow that dissolved the dew and sent the morning mists scurrying off the fields. Lying flat on the cool ground, Valentine said suddenly:

"Alec, give me your field-glasses."

He adjusted the lenses, gazed at the grey stable to the left of the Abbaye. Clearly he saw Baptiste walk out of the door, a long pegged rope in his hand. He saw him give a gentle tug at the rope and then he saw Venus follow slowly, ponderously. He saw her stop half-way through the door as if waiting to allow the brightness of the sunshine to filter leisurely into her fringed eyes, saw her consent to enter the day. She drank deeply at the water-butt, swishing her long tail in lazy contentment. Valentine handed the field-glasses to Alec with a grin. He took them and moved the slide a fraction and watched Baptiste lead Venus past the row of cottages to the fringe of grass. She walked slowly, her udder swinging deeply between slender legs and elegant ankles, the washed plume of her tail snow-white in the distance. Baptiste found a circle of rich grass and drove the steel peg into the ground with his heel, the staccato sound of each stamp taking a full second to reach their ears over the valley. Baptiste returned to the stable and Venus, blandly oblivious of the fact that she and her unborn calf were objects of interest equally to Whitehall and to the Wilhelmstrasse, put down her head and began to munch the grass of Armorel, with every manifestation of enjoyment.

As Nicola slipped into the copse, Valentine glanced round. She saw, not without a certain satisfaction, that there was a mixture of anxiety and relief in his eyes. He said to her, his mouth a hard line:

"You're late. You're seven minutes late."

She knew that he spoke sharply because of his disquiet. She sat down between him and Alec and put her handkerchief on the ground. It was rolled up into a bundle and tied with a knot. She sat clasping her knees, gazing in silence over the sunny valley.

"Sorry," she said at last. "I'm sorry I'm late. Not my fault. The Provost's wife made him change and put on his Sunday suit before he met me. It was all very grand. He even wore his watch-chain." She blinked. "Valentine, you don't know what it is to come home to people like these. I feel very humble. These people are the salt of the earth. You may count on the island absolutely, man, woman and child. We have three hundred allies on our side."

"I was as worried as hell. Weren't we, Alec?"

"You were, Mr. Valentine."

"Shall I be honest and tell you a shameless truth—that I knew you'd be worried? Shall I go even further and tell you that I now know myself to be a horrible woman at heart?"

"Why are you a horrible woman at heart?"

She gave him a sidelong glance.

"Because I was not really sorry that the Provost kept me waiting. That's why." Swiftly she changed the conversation. "Now may I tell you as much as I've found out?"

"Please do."

"I'm afraid that I'll want the map. Thank you, Valentine. After this we really can burn it—which will be a joy to us all." She spread it on the ground. "There *is* a German sentry on the *Pointe de Joie* from dusk to dawn and at these other points. By a miracle there isn't one at *Petit Pigeon* where we came in last night. These sentries are all connected up to German headquarters at the Abbaye by field telephone. Minefields are being sown here and here and here. There's a permanent garrison of about forty men—all English-speaking—and they're under the command of Captain Hans Weiss, who appears to be quite a decent chap. As we have the best of reasons for knowing, this Weiss person loves Venus dearly. That's complication number one. Complication number two is a man called Sergeant Vogel, who is a bully and a brute but who, I learn, is extremely observant. Practically nothing happens that he doesn't know about. Some three days ago a company of special troops arrived in the island to carry out some mysterious exercises. They are hand-picked Nazi thugs and there is no love lost between them and the garrison." She paused. "That may be useful to us or not."

"And what's complication number four?"

"It's the worst of the lot. There's a German gunboat called the *Lübeck* lying in the *Havre des Mouettes* and she's both fast and armed to the teeth."

"Oh," Valentine said slowly. "That's not too good."

"It's very bad."

There was silence between them, each of them examining this ominous information in a different light. Valentine saw it as the portent of the failure of a mission. He knew Uncle George fairly well and he knew that that hard and ruthless man would not hesitate. When he had handed Valentine the file, he had written on it "To Major Valentine Morland—for action. R.I.P." Uncle George waged war with all his strength and he would never risk the sacrifice of a ship to save their three lives. In the grand balance of the battle, that was fair enough. It did not occur to him to withhold the information from the War Office, but he had no doubt whatsoever as to what Uncle George's decision would be. He only wished with all his heart that Alec and he had come alone. . . . Nicola did not see her island any more. She saw on the screen of her mind a little ship on a vast sea and she saw a bigger ship that overhauled it scornfully, cutting off its escape. . . .

Alec was the first to speak. He said carefully:

"How do you spell the name of the ship, Mr. Valentine?"

"L-Ü-B-E-C-K. Why?"

"I want to get it right when I transmit at one o'clock."

"Well, now you know. In the meantime, we carry on as if nothing had happened. We simply forget that blasted gunboat or, if we can't do that, we pretend it isn't there. Alec, you will make your way over the route we still intend to take to-night, cut the telephone wire from the *Pointe de Joie* to the Abbaye and get the 'feel' of the land. I will head for the *Baie de l'Ondine* and prepare to-night's firework display, leaving here five minutes after you. You and I will meet again where we are now just before one so that you can fix your aerial and be ready to talk to London at one." He smiled. "And now, Nicola, how do you propose to spend your morning?"

"The Provost and I worked out an idea. Please, both of you, don't laugh. It may sound comic but it's deadly serious—and it's the only way we can get Venus from the top meadow. You know . . . the man I told you about, my cousin Lionel?"

"The long-haired pacifist painter?"

"Yes. The pacifist painter. His hair isn't particularly long. Well, listen . . ."

The Provost of Armorel went into the parlour of his cottage and shut the door. With deliberation he went down on his knees on the polished linoleum and clasped his hands and bent his head. For a long time he was motionless. Then he began to speak, his voice muffled in the quiet room.

"*Oh Dieu tout-puissant, Roi des rois . . . à la puissance duquel nulle créature ne peut résister . . . sauve nous ; étant couverts de ta protection, nous soyons garantis de tout danger, pour te glorifier, oh Dieu, qui seul donnes la victoire. . . .*"

The Provost stood up and went into the hall. He took his bowler hat from the antler hatstand and brushed it carefully on his sleeve. From the kitchen door, his wife watched him with fear in her eyes. She said timidly:

"Jacques . . . tell me, where are you going?"

Slowly he straightened his bent spine and stood upright.

"I am going about the business of my Suzerain and his sister," he said proudly.

Nicola was ready to go. She picked up the bundled handkerchief, holding it very carefully. Valentine said curiously:

"What have you got there?"

"You wouldn't guess in a thousand years. Coming over the *Clos d'Argent* from the Provost's house, I found three mushrooms. One for each of us. I thought we'd have them for breakfast to-morrow morning . . . in London."

Valentine looked at her steadily. "In London?"

"Yes. In London. Some people carry Saint Christophers. Well, these three mushrooms are from Armorel and they grew in my brother's field and they're my Saint Christophers."

She walked down the flank of the hill towards the road. Magpies flashed about the hedges in the morning sun, and over the far *Pointe de Joie* a kestrel hovered in the bright air. Valentine and Alec watched Nicola as she reached the valley, crossed it and began to mount the hill. She looked very small and very solitary, a tiny diminishing speck of white in her hand. Alec said drily:

"There goes to-morrow morning's breakfast, Mr. Valentine."

"There goes——" He stopped and swallowed. "Do you know what she told me in London? She said that she was out with this cousin Lionel of hers one September evening. They'd been fishing or something and were coming home in the dusk in a high wind bringing the rain with it from Sark. They took shelter and watched the rain come. Suddenly, she said, she knew that they were not alone. She said that a centaur galloped into the field where they were sheltering and pawed the ground, snorting, and then raced across the rocky field and leapt into the wind. She saw the sparks fly from its hoofs and she heard the hammer of its galloping. She said that her cousin saw these things too and they both knew it was a centaur. She told me this solemnly, in an air raid, sitting in a London restaurant, with hell's delight going on in the sky." He paused. "She isn't an ordinary sort of girl, Alec."

"I'd like her with me in trouble, Mr. Valentine."

"I'd like her with me any time. Alec, you'd better get moving. Good hunting to you."

"And to you, Mr. Valentine . . ."

CHAPTER FOURTEEN

BREATHING CANVAS

LIONEL FALLAIZE emerged with mounting resentment from the mists of sleep to the reality of another day. For a long time he lay with his eyes closed, unwilling to dispel the darkness in which the thronging images of his brain took shape and colour on the canvas of his mind. It was always in this motionless hour that his fingers mixed their most subtle pigment, in this hour that his greatest pictures were painted, in this silent hour that his greatest songs were sung. But where, this morning, were the bright children who usually came flocking? Where were the coloured balloons and where the radiance? There was grey on the canvas and black on his brush and things that he didn't want to gaze upon. He shook his head and opened his eyes. He was glad to see the sun.

He got out of bed, stretched and walked, his feet bare, into the messy kitchen. He filled a kettle and put it on the stove. While waiting for it to boil, he went into the living-room where he sat down and contemplated a half-finished painting on an easel. It was an ambitious work and one on which he had spent many weeks. From one corner, the gentle face of Christ looked with infinite melancholy on a turbulent riot of colour that dissolved into the grinning mask of a gorilla. Between the Godhead and the ape, there was a bridge across which half-formed figures of men and women desperately struggled. Lionel looked at the picture critically, saddened by the limitations of his fingers. If only, if only he could paint as he could see. . . .

He rose to his feet and opened the window wide. It was going to be a beautiful day. The dew was off the grass and already there was warmth in the sun. In the quietness of the morning he heard the sound of men's voices singing and then he saw the singers. It was a platoon of German soldiers returning to the Abbaye from whatever foul rendezvous they had kept in the hours of darkness. Theirs was not a song of the morning. It was a song of war and victory and death and the men shouted it, stamping their boots to its macabre chorus. Lionel watched the platoon pass. The soldiers were young and fit and blind and doomed and it seemed to him that they marched, shouting their blasphemies, into the mouth of a grave. And then he saw another thing. He saw a girl walking up the road alone. She moved to one side so that the marching column could pass and he saw the men's heads turn and he heard their obscene whistling like the whining of animals on heat. He saw her wave to them gaily and his lip curled in disgust. It was, at least, a suitable scene for inclusion in the half-finished canvas behind him, the impression of steel-helmeted skulls opening and shutting the dark caverns of their mouths while the immortal harlot grimaced and postured and cheered them on with bony, ringed fingers.

He shut the window and went back into the kitchen. The kettle was boiling. He began to make coffee, using a very little for his store was meagre and there was little chance of its being replenished. The smell of the bubbling coffee was pleasant in his nostrils and the jagged splinters of his ill-humour began to soften. It was at the moment when he was raising his cup to his lips that he heard his front door open and steps in the passage. They were confident steps, the steps of one who was entering a familiar place, and he recognized them instantly with a shock that drove the breath from his body.

He saw Nicola come into the kitchen. She smiled at him. His hand gripped the table so hard that his knuckles were white. She took a cup and saucer from the dresser and poured out some coffee. The cup rattled in the saucer and he knew that her fingers too were trembling. She sat down. She said unsteadily:

"You . . . you told me to come back soon from my bloody war. Well, I've come."

Valentine Morland took the narrow path that was cut into the cliff and wound down to the stretch of sand that was called *Baie de l'Ondine*, Mermaid Bay. He walked very quietly, his haversack slung over one shoulder. At a sharp turn of the path he stopped to eat a handful of blackberries. This simple act of picking blackberries in the September sunshine was so natural that he was conscious of a sense of complete unreality. Could it be true that he had landed on this island secretly by submarine? Could it be true that he was surrounded by enemies and that he, Nicola and Alec moved in mortal danger? He descended the path, his mood still upon him, and arrived at the sheltered beach. He put down his haversack and leaned against a rock and looked out to sea. There was a light sou'-wester blowing so that the bright surface of the water was restless and the far rocks were fringed with petticoats of foam. For many minutes he gladdened his eyes with what he saw and then, with a slight sigh, came back to the purposes of war. He took out his Colt automatic and laid it near to his hand. He unbuckled his haversack, and very carefully lifted out three explosive charges, setting the time pencils so that they would detonate at the appointed time one after the other at four-minute intervals. He buried the charges in the rough shape of a triangle, placing them high up in the sand out of the reach of the fingers of the sea. Then he came back to the shelter of the rock and took from his pocket a folding Zeiss Ikon camera. He focused it on the distant coastline and began to take photographs. He was in the act of winding on his seventh picture when he heard a slight sound behind him. He swung round on his heel, his hand snatching up his Colt and his thumb sliding the safety catch forward. A small ragged boy of about ten was watching him with a fixed, unblinking stare. In his hand he held a toy pistol and the tin barrel was pointing at Valentine's heart.

Valentine said, "Hullo."

Very slowly, inch by inch, he raised his hands above

his head. He did it very solemnly. With death in his right hand, he yielded to death's image.

The boy said nothing. Around him Valentine could hear the surge and ebb of the sea, and above him, the intermittent flurry of the wind in the gorse. The silence between them deepened. He said again:

"Hullo."

The live cartridges of Valentine's Colt fitted snugly into their oiled chambers, waiting only for the touch of his finger to send them banging and tearing and ripping into the boy's flesh. The tin barrel, its sections bound together with string, was very steady. The boy spoke. He said in a queer, sing-song voice:

"I saw you come last night, you and Miss Nicola and your friend. I live in the house of my uncle Pierre. The Provost is my grandfather. You crossed the farm of my uncle. I was not asleep. I saw you."

"That's a pity. We should have been more careful. May I put my hands down?"

"Yes. You may put them down. But I still have my pistol. I warn you that I still have my pistol."

"You are very kind." He lowered his arms. "What is your name?"

"Why should I tell you? What is *your* name?"

"Why should *I* tell you?"

"Because it is I who have the pistol. That is why."

"I had overlooked that. My name is Valentine."

"Mine is Georges."

"Now we know each other."

"Yes." The boy went on calmly, stating without

emphasis what he knew to be true, "Miss Nicola has been to my grandfather and is now gone to see Mr. Lionel. He is mad but all right. Your friend—I don't know his name—is near the *Pointe de Joie*. He is clever and in a good place where the Germans won't see him. He is more clever than you, Monsieur Valentine. You are in a very bad place."

"Oh. Why am I in a very bad place?"

"Because from here there is only one path. There is no escape for you when the Germans come."

"But why should the Germans come?"

"Because they come every day at this time when the weather is good to swim in the sea. To-day the weather is good."

"My God!"

"It is a bad thing to say 'my God'. If I say 'my God' my grandfather beats me."

"Your grandfather is quite right," he said absently, "and I should like to meet him. One of the nineteenth-century virtues was corporal punishment for the young. I think it is high time I got out of here."

"So do I." Georges suddenly lifted his head and listened intently. He said breathlessly, "But you are too late. Listen! The Germans are coming."

Into the quietness slid the sound of men's voices singing in German. The chorus came from the top of the path and it surged in the flurries of the wind, coming nearer and nearer. Georges stamped his bare foot in the sand.

"Quickly, Monsieur Valentine. There is only one

thing. You must swim with the Germans. I will take your clothes . . . and everything . . . and meet you round the headland. Swim there to me."

Valentine tore off his jersey, wrapped his Colt and his haversack in its folds, kicked off his shoes. The chorus was louder and louder, filling the air with menace. He stripped off his trousers, flung them to Georges, ran naked across the sand. At the moment when the leading German rounded the last bend of the path, Valentine launched his body into the sea in a smother of foam. He swam strongly out from shore. Fifty yards out, he trod water and looked back. One of the Germans, an N.C.O., was shouting at Georges.

"You, it is not permitted to come to the sea. What are you doing?"

"Waiting for the English to land, of course."

Valentine heard his guffaw of laughter. "*Du bist frech, Du!* You will wait a long time. Don't let Sergeant Vogel catch you, that's all. Who is that swimming?"

"You think you are the only people on Armorel!" Georges said with reverence. "That is without doubt Mister Winston Churchill."

"*Ach so.* Then I am Hermann Göring."

The men were undressing, folding their clothes into neat bundles. Three of them raced towards the breaking foam, flung themselves into the curling waves. Valentine put his face into the water and began to swing his arms into a slow, powerful crawl. Within a minute his head was indistinguishable from those of the shouting swimmers. Once he looked back towards the shore. Half-way up the cliff-path he saw a tiny figure trudging with a bundle, saw the figure stop by a bend. He chuckled. He hoped that Georges was enjoying the blackberries as much as he had.

Lionel leaned against the table and stared at Nicola. He was in blue silk pyjamas and his feet were bare. She put down her cup. She said calmly:

"Hadn't you better put on a dressing-gown and some slippers? Your feet'll get jolly cold."

"I haven't got any slippers. Nicola, may I touch you?"

"Of course."

She stretched out her hand. He took her fingers in his, held them and let them go.

"Yes. You really are here. If I go and put a dressing-gown on, you won't have vanished by the time I get back, will you?"

"No. I promise to stay."

He went into his bedroom, put on a dark blue dressing-gown, came back. She was still in the kitchen. She said to him: "Haven't you really got any slippers, Lionel?"

"No. But I'll find something. Don't go."

"What do you think I'm going to do? Disappear up the chimney on a broomstick? Or jump into the wind, like the centaur?"

"You might."

He went back into his bedroom and put on the first things he could find, a pair of Wellingtons. She had poured herself out a second cup of coffee by the time he came back. She looked very cool and composed, sitting calmly by the stove. It seemed to him that she had never been away from Armorel at all and that the year that had passed had gone like the flight of an angry bee. He said to her:

"It was you who waved to the soldiers, wasn't it?"

"Yes. It was me. I couldn't avoid them so it seemed the best thing to do. Sorry."

"I'm sorry too. Not that you waved at them but . . . but that I thought meanly of you. I didn't know it was you. Nicky, where have you come from and what are you doing here?"

Time for her, too, was the tick of the clock. It was surely only yesterday that they had climbed the church tower together—and the day before that when, as a little girl, she had nailed two champagne corks on to the flat heels of her sandals, wrapped herself in the nursery curtains and told her nurse that she might be a little late for tea as she was off to marry her cousin Lionel. . . . And yet more than a year had passed since she had bidden him good-bye. He was thinner than he had been and the restlessness in his hands and in his eyes was more marked. She had an almost irresistible desire to stand up and walk over to him and smooth away the furrows of his brow with her hand. . . .

"Where have I come from and what am I doing here? I've come from London. I was in London yesterday. I saw your mother but she couldn't send you her love because I couldn't tell her that I was coming home. She thinks I've gone to Tokio. We came in a submarine and landed at *Petit Pigeon* some time after midnight."

" 'We'? Who came? Nicola . . . are you mad? The Germans are here."

"I know. That's why we had to come by submarine and land in darkness. Two people came with me, a man called Valentine Morland and another man called Alexander Forbes, who is a radio operator. At this moment Valentine is preparing to-night's firework display at the *Baie de l'Ondine* and Alec is somewhere between here and the *Pointe de Joie*. You remember Trawler Langley? Well, Trawler took us inshore last night in a rubber dinghy, had a scout round and then went back to England. He's collecting us to-night, not in a submarine, but in a thing called an M.T.B." She paused. She said innocently, "You see, cows don't fit into submarines."

Lionel stood up, ran his fingers through his hair, sat down again. He said imperiously:

"Nicola, tell."

"We've come to collect Venus, Luke's pedigree Guernsey. As you know, she's heavily in calf to the late-lamented Mars and Whitehall doesn't want that calf to fall into German hands. It's much too valuable, not in money, which doesn't matter, but to English pedigree breeding—which matters a lot. We don't want it to grow up into a foul little Nazi bull, heiling and mooing and lording it over other calves. If it's a heifer, we want it simply to be a heifer and not a vicious little Hitler *Mädel* with flaxen plaits and hatred in her heart.

That part of it's quite simple. The trouble is that the Commandant, Captain Weiss, is so attached to Venus that he won't let her out of his sight." She glanced at him from under her lashes. "That is where you come in, Lionel."

"What do you mean?"

"I mean what I say. We want your help."

"I don't begin to understand." His thin face hardened. "And I warn you that I will do violence to no man. Not even for you, Nicky."

The ghost of a smile flitted across her lips. She stood up, slim and lissom and utterly desirable in his eyes. She said gently:

"No one is going to ask you to do violence . . . to a man." She glanced through the half-open door to the living-room. "May I see what you've been painting? You used to let me look."

"Of course."

She stood in silence before the easel. He took her hand in his and held it tightly. He was filled with wonder and with unbelief that the cool fingers resting between his should be Nicola's fingers, their movement directed by Nicola's brain, their skin Nicola's skin and their nails Nicola's nails. At this moment he asked for no more than that he should continue to touch her hand and to know that she was breathing beside him. She said slowly:

"That's the best thing you've ever done, Lionel." She turned impulsively and faced him. "It makes what I want to say to you very difficult. I know that there's only one step between the sublime and the ridiculous, so will you bear with me?"

"Of course. What do you want me to do, darling Nicola?"

She drew a deep breath. "I want you to paint a cow to look like Venus."

A man in a blue jersey trudged along the road past the open window and glanced incuriously into the living-room. He half-stopped and scratched his head, walked slowly on. Nicola said quickly:

"Come into the kitchen. We can be seen here."

Lionel followed her into the kitchen. She said to him in a rush of words:

"Please don't think I'm mad. I've been to see the Provost already and we worked out this together. There's only one way we can get Venus away from that top pasture and that is by substituting an inferior cow painted to resemble her markings. I know the time when Captain Weiss has lunch and it's about then that I would change her over. Provided he doesn't look at the newcomer too closely, we should get away with it. Then we hide up the real Venus until dark and inveigle her gently down to the *Pointe de Joie*." She took a step forward and put her two hands on his shoulders. "I thought that was a jolly good scheme until I saw what you really can paint. Now I'm ashamed." She blinked. "If you don't want to do it, say so, and I promise you that I'll understand."

He looked at her excited face and into her clear, shining eyes. He had no desire to kiss her mouth or take her pliant body in his arms. He only wanted to go on looking at her so that her image should be etched on his mind for ever. He said huskily:

"Darling Nicola."

"And darling Lionel . . ."

"Are you glad to be home?"

"Very. No matter what happens, I'm glad to be home."

"And I'm . . . very glad to see you." He shook his head and his lean face was suddenly illuminated by the schoolboy grin she used to know so well. He said, "Wait." He went into the living-room, came back with a paint-box, brushes and tubes.

"Now let's see. I've got yellow ochre, Chinese white and burnt sienna. They should do. Of course, the surface isn't like canvas. It's all hairy. The thing I really need is poster paint—or better still, distemper."

"Then you'll do it?"

"Mademoiselle," he said grandly, "I accept your commission. There was a French symbolist in the 'nineties who painted scenes from the Garden of Eden on the skin of his pet python and then took it for walks —or should I say wriggles?—in the Bois, leading it on a chain of fig leaves. The true artist disdains the limitations of surface. The first thing for me to do is to make some sketches of the real Venus's markings. Where is she now?"

"Pegged out in front of the Abbaye in the top pasture. While you're making your notes, I'll go and . . . er . . . borrow one of old Mrs. Guilleaume's more placid cows and bring her here. Then we can get busy on the great transformation. Lionel, isn't this fun? It's like when we were little."

"Yes—but the penalty for being found out would be heavier. We'd get more than a spanking. Be very careful, darling Nicola."

"I will, darling Lionel." She paused. "Do you know, I've never called a man 'darling' in my life. Not even you until now. And we've known each other for so long."

"We've known each other always. Do you remember what was on the bell?"

"Yes. I remember."

"Ours is a *Maison éternelle*, Nicola."

"I know. May I do something before I go?"

"What?"

"Make your bed. I'd like to. And then I want to find one more mushroom. I've got three already."

"What do you want a fourth mushroom for?"

"Breakfast in London to-morrow morning, Lionel."

Valentine Morland, every muscle in his body aching from his long swim, walked unsteadily from the sea and up the shingle. He sat down naked in the sand and breathed deeply, his head between his knees.

"You swim very well, Monsieur Valentine."

"I'm glad you think so, Georges. May I have my trousers?"

From his perch on a spit of rock, Georges threw the trousers and Valentine caught them deftly. Valentine put them on and stood up. There were bright drops of sea water on his shoulders and he rubbed his numbed fingers together.

"Now my shirt, please."

There was a chuckle of pure delight. Valentine looked up. The boy Georges was sitting cross-legged on the rock. In his hand he held Valentine's Colt and its deadly barrel was aimed at Valentine's left breast. He said, his eyes alight with mischief:

"Monsieur Valentine, you were foolish. The pistol I had before was not a real one. It was only a toy. But this is a real one."

"I am aware of it," said Valentine. "I am sharply aware of it. It is also loaded."

"Oh, how wonderful. Monsieur, may I please fire one shot? Please."

Valentine swallowed.

"I wouldn't do that if I were you. Honestly I wouldn't. Not just now anyway. Yours is a much finer pistol than mine, much finer in every way. Won't you do a swop?"

"But I have done a swop."

"Well, then, do a re-swop." He moved discreetly out of the direction of the barrel. "When I get back to England I'll send you some Guatemalan stamps as well. I'll even include a mouse's skeleton."

With a sigh Georges handed him the pistol and he promptly slid the catch back to safety. He sat down and, in considerable relief, began to put on his shoes and stockings and his jersey.

"You won't tell a living soul that you've seen Miss Nicola, or my friend, or me, will you, Georges?"

"Do you think I am an imbecile, Mr. Valentine?"

"No, I don't. I think you're a brave boy and a good, good comrade. That's what I think. And I also think that the Germans may find out, after I've gone, what you've done to help me and that then there would be a lot of trouble for you. Georges, would you like to come to England with me?"

"Oh, yes, monsieur, please take me to England. Please, monsieur."

"Listen to me very carefully, Georges. If you really want to come to England with me, with us, be at the *Point de Joie* at exactly a quarter past ten to-night. If . . . anything happens and we don't go, you can return home and no harm done."

"I understand. May I take my pistol with me to England?"

"Yes—if you promise not to fire it."

"I promise. Now I will go."

Suddenly Georges was gone as if he had vanished into the bright air. Valentine took a deep breath and whistled. He looked up the cliff, searching for the route with the best cover. The boy's voice spoke behind him.

"Monsieur Valentine."

"Yes, Georges."

An emotion struggled in Georges' face, found utterance in a stammered, long-familiar phrase.

He said, "God save the King."

CHAPTER FIFTEEN

TREE IN BLOOM

JEAN "la Bouteille", the Thirsty One, had been a member of the Court of Armorel for many years. He was a man of nearly sixty and the delicate labyrinth of blue veins that spread over his weather-beaten face was evidence that he had, in the past if not in the present, well deserved his jovial nickname. In the evening of the day the Germans had first come to Armorel and in the presence of his friends of the Court he had made a solemn undertaking—that no drop of alcohol would pass his lips until such time as he could raise his glass to the return of his Suzerain. He had given his promise in the name of God and he had kept to it. He had kept to it through long, restless nights when he lay under his blankets staring into the darkness, the thirsty tissues of his flesh tingling for the solace of the grape. An added torment was the presence in the parlour cupboard of a bottle of French brandy. He would look at it sometimes and take it off the shelf, caressing it, while his tongue curled up to the roof of his mouth and his glands oozed at the imagined sight of the corkscrew's prong wriggling deeply into the cork and the cork being withdrawn, very slowly and carefully, until it emerged from the reluctant neck of the bottle with a soft plop and the sweet smell of the breathing spirit tangled itself in the hairs of his nostrils. At this point, he would put the bottle back hurriedly and lock the cupboard and go out to the yard and take a spade or a pitchfork in his hands and banish, in strenuous physical exertion, the devil that slumbered in his bloodstream.

He was a simple, honourable man with a care for his word.

On this fine September morning, he left his cottage to go to his work on the roads. The leaves of autumn had already begun to fall and the gutters on the steep *Colline des Mouettes* were choked so that the rivulets of water welled up and trickled and flowed over the road. He passed the open door of the *Estaminet des Anges* and saw a little group of German soldiers sitting round the scrubbed table where he had spent so many convivial hours in the days and nights when Armorel was free and the Suzerain walked his own fields. The Germans were drinking what passed for coffee and even at this early hour they had ordered Cognac to wash down the thin, tasteless liquid. One of them saw the old man trudging to work and raised his glass in mocking salutation. He called out, laughing:

"Good morning, Jean. *Prosit.* You wish to join us in a glass?"

"*Non merci, messieurs.*" He shrugged and gave a toothless grin. "*Non merci, messieurs.*"

He walked on, quickening his pace to get away from the open door with its glimpse of the clean tables and wooden chairs, the counter and the shelves behind where the labelled bottles stood, coloured dark green and brown, each one of them whispering. The German scrambled to his feet and went to the door. He shouted:

"Jean . . . Jean."

Jean la Bouteille turned round and looked at the smiling German with great dignity. "Monsieur?"

"Come. I wish to speak with you. Come."

Jean walked back heavily. The tantalizing smell of centuries of potation was about the open door and he stood to one side. The German, conscious of the attention of his comrades, grinned broadly.

"When I invited you to join us in a glass, you replied in the French language. That is forbidden. You also refused. That too is forbidden. I now invite you once more for a glass. If you do not accept, I will feel it my duty to report to our good Sergeant Vogel that you speak insults to the German garrison in the French language." He clicked his heels. "Jean—you are invited for a glass. Come."

Jean gazed at him. He put down his brush and spade and walked deliberately into the bar. The smell mounted in his nose like fire. He approached the counter and looked glassily at his old friend Charles, who wiped his hands on his apron and stared at the floor with downcast eyes. Jean said thickly:

"I will take a bottle of lemonade with the German gentleman, Charles. Yes, a bottle of lemonade. You heard, eh? Give it to me quickly. For the love of God, give quickly . . ."

He raised his glass and faced the Germans.

"You are very kind," he said. "*Santé, messieurs.*"

He drank it at a gulp and walked out into the morning, his nostrils twitching. He took the road that led past Mr. Lionel's house. These Germans were *salauds, salauds, salauds . . . cochons et salauds*! He walked on muttering, hardly realizing the direction he took. Drunken pigs, that's what they were. *Sales Boches*. . . . He breathed deeply as he walked, for there was a smell in his lungs that filled him with fear and he must rid his body of an evil thing. *Notre Père, qui es aux Cieux . . . et ne nous induis point en tentation, mais delivrons du mal*. . . . Now he was passing Mr. Lionel's house. He glanced at the open window of the living-room. Mr. Lionel was there, talking to a lady. He saw them clearly and half-stopped. It was none of his business if Mr. Lionel talked to ladies. Mr. Lionel was his own master, and could talk to whom he liked. Not that he did ever talk to ladies—except Miss Nicola. That had been common talk on Armorel, that Mr. Lionel had no eyes for anyone other than Miss Nicola and that Miss Nicola had only eyes for Mr. Lionel. Like children they had been, walking hand in hand——

Jean stopped dead. He stared, his mouth open, at the sky. The lady Mr. Lionel had been talking to was Miss Nicola. It *was* Miss Nicola. It was the sister of the Suzerain. The wheels of his mind revolved slowly and then what seemed to be a great and blinding truth suddenly burst on his brain. Miss Nicola had come home. There could only be one reason. The war was over and Armorel was free, free, free. . . .

Jean let his brush and spade fall to the ground. He stumbled back the way he had come. The door of his cottage was shut but he kicked it open with his heavy boots. This was no occasion for a corkscrew and his dream of slowly mounting delight dissolved like mist before the sun. He took the bottle of Cognac and drove the cork down with his thumb and spilled out a gurgling, amber stream that nearly filled a kitchen cup. The cork bobbed gaily on the imprisoned liquid and it splashed as he set the bottle with a crash on the kitchen table. He lifted the cup and the next instant his gullet was working and gulping and a slow fire began to glow and to spread in the parched membrane of his stomach.

Venus grazed placidly on the crest of the hill in front of the Abbaye. Sitting against a tree, a drawing-pad on his knees, Lionel Fallaize made a rough pencil sketch of her, shading in her brown and golden markings. The artist within him was unable to resist the temptation to put in the sweep of the plough behind her and its geometrical furrows. He was darkening the shadows where the gorse began when the door of the Abbaye opened and Captain Weiss came out. He walked across to Lionel and said politely:

"Good morning, Mr. Fallaize. You permit me to see?"

"Why not?"

He handed the drawing-pad to Captain Weiss, who looked at it with mounting enthusiasm, glancing critically from the sketch to its subject. At last he handed it back with a chuckle.

"Mr. Fallaize, I congratulate you. All of a moment you have become a realist and your style has changed. This is so much better than your angular landscapes and your sunsets seen through bars. Out of ten thousand pictures of cows, I would know this for Venus." He looked over Lionel's shoulder at the drawing again, his head on one side. He frowned. "There is one thing."

"Oh? Do tell me."

"It is with deference that a soldier makes a suggestion to an artist, but you have drawn her from the left side. On her right flank there is a mark like . . . like a tree in bloom. It is quite distinctive. If my fingers had the skill of yours, I would draw her from over there."

"The artist," said Lionel, "gladly accepts the suggestion of the soldier. In all representative art, one should seek the distinctive and the characteristic. You remember Cromwell's wart?"

"Cromwell's wart? No, I know nothing of this."

"It's a historical parallel." He stood up smiling, and walked to a point where he could view Venus from the right. Weiss followed him. He said regretfully:

"You are no doubt aware that the Reichsamt for Agriculture in Berlin has ordered that Venus be sent to Germany where she will bear her calf."

"Venus," said Lionel drily, "appears to be a very popular lady. Er . . . when does she leave?"

"At any hour. It is only a question of transport."

"I wouldn't send her away to-day if I were you. There is a distinct swell at sea and you know yourself that she is in a delicate state of health. Much better to send her to-morrow." He began to work with his pencil. Weiss said cautiously:

"You remember, Mr. Fallaize, that you once said you would like to present me with a picture, a picture without bars?"

"I do indeed remember."

"Well, this, the drawing you are doing, is of such a kind. I would be very proud to have it framed and to hang it by the Mess fireplace. Then I would always remember not only Venus herself but you, the man who immortalized her. Why, Mr. Fallaize, you are laughing! Never before have I known you to laugh. I am very glad to see that you are capable of laughter. Yes, I am very glad."

Nicola walked unobtrusively along the grass track that led to old Mrs. Guilleaume's farm. The Provost was waiting for her at a bend of the hedge and at her approach he swept off his bowler hat. She smiled.

"It's all arranged. He'll do it."

"I never doubted it. Mr. Lionel is, before anything else, one of us. Now look, Miss Nicola, that's the one I meant."

In Mrs. Guilleaume's field, four cows were grazing. The Provost pointed to the nearest one, a lightish animal with amber markings and incurving horns.

"That's Hyacinth, isn't it?"

"Yes. She's eight months in calf to Star Prince."

"Her horns are wrong and we can't change them. We can do the rest." She looked critically at the animal and nodded. "Well, if you'll go now and occupy Mrs. Guilleaume's attention for ten minutes, I'll take up my new rôle of cattle thief. And then we'll meet later, as arranged."

"Very well, Miss Nicola."

Although the Provost was once to see her again in peculiar circumstances, she gazed on his face for the last time in her life.

Looking very conscious of his office, the Provost knocked on the door of the farmhouse. Mrs. Guilleaume came from the kitchen and greeted him warmly. To her surprise he answered her with unaccustomed formality and produced from his pocket a bundle of official schedules for her immediate attention. She led the way into the parlour and Nicola saw the door of the farmhouse shut behind her. Quickly she brushed through the hedge and into the field.

Hyacinth looked up from her grazing in mild curiosity. She made no attempt to move away as Nicola loosened the steel peg of her rope. She was used to being moved periodically to a new circle of grass and followed without protest, across the field, through the gate and on to the twisting lane. Within a matter of minutes, Nicola led her into Lionel's backyard, shut the door and sat down on an upturned bucket to await her cousin's return. She had not seen a living soul on the way and she was filled with exhilaration. Surely the gods who had flung a falling star to watch over them wouldn't desert them now.

Jean la Bouteille sat down heavily in the tasselled armchair by the stove and stared blearily at the wall. In one hand he held a bottle that had very recently been full of French brandy. In his other hand he held a kitchen cup. Both the bottle and the cup were empty, but Jean's brain was full, full of brandy and delight and triumph and rage. He tried to stand up but his quivering knees refused to support him. He threw the cup into the grate, smashing it into fragments, and gripped the table with his free hand. Still he lurched back. The empty bottle followed the cup. It made a fine, brave noise as it splintered and the liberated cork rolled derisively back to his feet. He seized the table and heaved himself upright. He had one desire in his mind and one only. Swaying, he stumbled to the door and out into the fresh air. He wanted to shout to the sky but all he could do was mumble and retch as the brandy flamed like a furnace in his throat and in his stomach. He half-shambled and half-ran towards that building whose image had tormented him over the past parched weeks. Through glazed eyes he saw the open door of the *Estaminet des Anges* and the little group of German soldiers standing up to go, putting on their belts and caps. He thrust his way through them to the bar and swung round on his heel. There was a moment's frozen silence. Then Jean's voice came back to him in a strangled roar.

"Sit down, gentlemen, sit down. How many of you are there, *salauds, sales Boches*? How many. Answer me, *salauds*."

A corporal said quietly, looking at him with narrowed eyes:

"Have a care what you say, you drunken old fool."

"Me? Why should I have a care for *salauds*. How many of you?"

"We are six."

"Six! *Très bien.* Now it is the turn of the German gentlemen to drink with me." He turned round, reeling, to the stupefied barman Charles. "Give the German gentlemen six bottles of lemonade, and for me, Charles, brandy. Brandy, you hear. I command these *sales Boches* to drink with me to victory and to the return of Miss Nicola Fallaize, sister of the Suzerain of Armorel. . . ."

As the Provost left Mrs. Guilleaume's farmhouse, he looked at the field. Where four cows had grazed, there were now only three. He smiled gently to himself as he walked along the lane. The day went well.

He left the lane to join the road and saw a woman hurrying towards him. He recognized her at once. It was Françoise, the wife of Charles who kept the *Estaminet des Anges*, and he was astonished to see that she had come out in her apron. She waved to him frantically and came running, her face distraught and her mouth gabbling.

"*Monsieur le Provost*, come at once. A terrible thing . . . oh, a terrible thing."

"Françoise, what is it?"

"It is Jean, Jean la Bouteille. He is in the *Anges* and

he is drunk. He is shouting that Miss Nicola has come back to Armorel and that the war is over. He says that he has seen Miss Nicola with his own eyes!"

The Provost said quickly, "Is there anyone else there?"

"But yes. There are Germans, six of them. Jean shouts at them that the war is over and that the sister of the Suzerain is back."

The Provost passed his hand wearily across his face. He felt old—old and sick and weak.

"Go back now to the *Anges*. Tell your husband to wait in the yard until I bring Jean to him. Then he must strike so that Jean's mouth is shut. He must strike hard."

"But . . . but, *Monsieur le Provost*, you do not understand how it is with Charles. He has arms of iron and . . . and Jean might die from his blow."

"Then that would be the will of God. Charles must strike—hard and sure. Now go."

The brightness had faded from the sun. With eyes that took in nothing of the glory of that September morning, the Provost walked slowly, deliberately to betray his friend. There was no hesitation in his mind but only infinite sorrow for he knew clearly where his duty lay. It was with a sense of finality that he saw the open door of the *Estaminet des Anges* and the silent knot of German soldiers staring intently at the travesty of a man at the counter, a creature with a glass in its hand, a creature who mumbled and dribbled. The Provost walked into the room. Françoise was behind the counter and there was fear in her eyes. Charles had gone. . . .

The group of German soldiers loosened to admit him. He looked steadily at Jean. The glazed eyes focused with difficulty and the flushed face dissolved into a grin. The loose mouth slobbered and spoke.

"*C'est toi. C'est Jacques le Cheminant!*"

"No. It is not Jacques le Cheminant. It is the Provost of Armorel." He drew breath, and said in a voice of thunder, "I repeat, it is the Provost of Armorel."

Nobody moved. The only sound in the tense silence was that of Jean's heavy breathing. The Provost said very quietly, his voice instinct with authority:

"Jean, I order you to come with me."

The German soldiers fell back. The Provost turned on his heel and walked to the door. Jean followed him, swaying. The Provost led the way into the fresh air, turned to the right, opened a barred gate into a yard where a man waited, the broken spoke of a farm cart in his terrible hands. The Provost turned and faced Jean. His eyes were full of compassion. He tried to speak, but he could find no word. He looked at Charles and nodded once. There was a sound, a sickening sound like a butcher splitting a shin bone. The earth and the sky exploded in Jean's bemused brain and a scarlet web of blood flowed into his jersey as he sank to his knees like a stricken animal and rolled over and lay still.

Hyacinth stood calm and docile in Lionel's backyard while Nicola fed her sparingly with parsnips. Lionel, dressed professionally in his artist's smock, worked steadily on her left side, covering her brown markings with a wash of white, glancing every now and then for reference at his sketch of Venus. At last he stood back, his head on one side.

"Well, Nicola, what do you think of that?"

She gave Hyacinth a particularly large parsnip and came over and stood beside him.

"I think it's wonderful. Picasso will have to look to his laurels."

"I find the whole thing slightly surrealist. You being here . . . me painting a cow. I keep having to remind myself of the penalty of being found out and then I know it's true. When you get Venus away, where are you going to hide her up till darkness?"

"I don't know. I hadn't thought."

"Then you'd better bring her here and we'll keep her in my living-room." He chuckled. "There is, after all, a certain merit in being considered an eccentric, and nobody would think of looking for a pedigree cow in among the easels and the armchairs."

"Supposing somebody did look?"

"Then I'd rather she were found here than anywhere else." He looked at her solemnly. "Wouldn't you?"

"I don't want anyone on the island to be involved. I want nobody on Armorel to have to suffer after we've gone. That's why we're taking you home with us,

Lionel. Mushrooms for breakfast to-morrow morning and don't you forget it."

There could be no life for him on Armorel after this. The part that he had played would inevitably be discovered and German vengeance would follow swiftly and painfully. But what lay before him in the fortress of England where every man, woman and child braced themselves for the struggle? What place had he, a man with paint on his hand, amongst those who had blood on theirs? To have been allowed to share in this adventure was a full and a rich thing. Let it suffice.

He said easily:

"How do you cook your mushrooms?"

"Any way you like. Fried—or done with cream."

"It sounds perfect. Now, darling Nicola, will you please carry on with the parsnips while I start in on the right side. The expression used by my friend, Hans Weiss, was 'like a tree in bloom'."

CHAPTER SIXTEEN

UNCLE GEORGE AND THE DRAGON

IN the underground receiving room at the War Office the telegraphist glanced at the clock and at the man beside her.

"One minute to go and Valentine should be coming up." He adjusted his earphones and listened, his pencil poised. On the stroke of one o'clock, a gentle chatter sounded in his ears. He listened, gave the "am receiving you loud and clear" sign and began to write.

At ten minutes past one, a Royal Signals messenger tapped on the door of Room 057, entered, saluted, handed Uncle George a sealed envelope, saluted and went out. Uncle George tore the envelope open and began to read.

FOR UNCLE GEORGE FROM VALENTINE ALL WELL WITH ALL FOUR REPEAT FOUR OF US BUT MUST RELUCTANTLY REPORT PRESENCE IN HARBOUR OF FAST HEAVILY ARMED GUNBOAT LÜBECK STOP AM ALSO WORRIED ABOUT PRIMA DONNA'S CONDITION STOP IF OPERATION TO CONTINUE SUGGEST GENTLEMAN WITH LITTLE BLACK BAG MEETS US AT PORT OF ENTRY STOP WILL RECONTACT FIFTEEN HUNDRED HOURS G.M.T. FOR INSTRUCTIONS AND OR VALEDICTORY BLESSINGS ENDS.

Uncle George rubbed his chin and smiled. It was a human weakness to feel a certain sense of satisfaction when things worked out according to plan. On the other hand, the accelerated confinement of Venus was an event which he had been unable to prognosticate. The middle-aged secretary looked round incuriously from her typewriter. He said to her:

"Care to see this? It's from Valentine."

"Yes, I'd like to."

She was a plump little woman with mouse-coloured hair and a mouse-coloured dress. She had worked for Uncle George in peace as in war and she knew the inflexible, undeviating purpose in his mind. It was the defeat of the King's Enemies by whatever power or by whatever instrument, human or mechanical, that might come to his hand. An Army Commander flung his men and his armour into the battle when the enemy had been bewildered and bemused by a cannonade from the land and from the sky. Uncle George worked in silence and in twilight. He gave the men and women who went about his business no benefit of previous bombardment. He sent them on their perilous journeys alone. He offered them fear as their companion and death as their reward, death far from home, death by the bullet, the rope or the gas-chamber. He told them little other than the details of the particular job they had to do, and they went to it, unaware of its real purpose or how it fitted into the labyrinth of war that lay behind Uncle George's eyes. Some of them came back—to start off again on a new mission and a new loneliness. Others failed to return and eventually a little red seal was stuck on their personal files and the files were transferred from Uncle George's steel cabinet to another resting place. It was then that the middle-aged secretary would type the formal heart-breaking letter that began:

"Dear Madam: It is with the deepest regret that I must inform you that your son . . . or your daughter . . . or your husband . . ."

She put down Valentine's message. She said without apparent emotion:

"That's bad luck on Valentine and the other two. Shall I get you Portsmouth on the telephone?"

"What for?"

She glanced at him, surprised at his question. "To cancel the pick-up, of course."

"No," he said, "don't do that." He went on with seeming irrelevance, "How long have you worked for me now?"

"Quite a long time, Uncle George. Quite a long time enough to know that you're not going to send an M.T.B. and her crew to certain destruction for the sake of two men, a young woman and a cow."

"True." He smiled. He was well pleased with himself. "Tell me, have you ever read Kipling's 'Stalky & Co.'?"

"Yes. Years ago. Why?"

He quoted, looking at her over his spectacles:

" 'The bleating of the kid excites the tiger'? Does that mean anything to you?"

"I remember it. But I don't see the connection."

"Let me put it another way. 'The mooing of the cow excites the gunboat.' Now do you understand?"

She looked at him with curiosity. After all these years, she was still capable of being surprised by the workings of this extraordinary man's mind and by his innate guile. She said at last:

"Then you knew all the time that there was a fast gunboat in the harbour?"

"Yes, I knew. She's the latest thing in E-boats and she's put into Armorel for secret trials. She's a prototype and, please God, there'll be a lot of head-scratching in the Marine-Amt in Berlin to-morrow morning. The *Havre des Mouettes* is land-locked and she's safe as long as she stays in harbour. So we've got to entice her to come out. Once she's out—enter the R.A.F."

"May I ask you something?"

"You may ask."

"How did you know she was there?"

"There's no harm in my telling you now. I had the information from Stockholm last week and Stockholm had it direct from Kiel, from Otto. The Gestapo have caught up with Otto, poor devil, and we won't be hearing from him any more." He paused. "Because I am a sentimentalist I like to think that we were making the best possible use of his last message. I didn't like Otto much. He wore a hair-net and stays and boasted of his successes with women. But he was full of guts."

"I didn't know about his hair-net. May I ask you something else?"

"Ask on."

"Why didn't you tell Valentine about the gunboat? It wouldn't have made any difference to him. He would have gone just as willingly."

"I know. But he would have found some means of leaving Nicola Fallaize behind and she was essential. I know Valentine. He has old-fashioned ideas about women and danger. He didn't like doing what he did in Lisbon and he needed what he thought was a holiday from war to restore his balance. Operation Venus isn't Battle à la Butlins but it's his social equivalent of it. It's bird-watching on the grand scale—with a cause added on. If a man like Valentine is going to risk his life anyway, why not give him a thing he believes in to risk it for?"

"So you offered him a pedigree cow when you really wanted an E-boat?"

"I want the pedigree cow too. Valentine and the cow are now inseparable."

"How so?"

"Listen," he said patiently. "I knew that he'd report back the presence of that E-boat even though he thought I'd ditch the whole thing and leave him to find his own way home. That's what I think of my friend Major Valentine Morland. He's the best argument I know in favour of the higher education. He'll either get Venus and her calf home or you'll have to type one of your letters beginning 'Dear Madam'. Have you got your note-book?"

"Yes, Uncle George."

"Right. Get this message over to Signals for transmission at once. FOR VALENTINE FROM UNCLE GEORGE DON'T BE A BF OPERATION CONTINUES AS PLANNED ENDS. Then I want the Ops. Room of Fighter Command on the scrambler and the Admiralty Charts of Armorel. You'll find Trawler Langley restricting himself to a dry ginger ale in the Silver Cross and I want to see him before he goes down again to Portsmouth. When you've done all that, get me the Deputy Director of the Army Veterinary Corps and order a fast car to stand by for an urgent journey to the coast. All clear?"

"All clear, Uncle George."

He picked up Valentine's message, read it again, and snorted.

"Valedictory blessings indeed. Who the hell does he think I am?"

"None of us know," said the secretary sadly.

CHAPTER SEVENTEEN

THE HUNT IS UP

THE falling star had them still under its protection. A mass of official papers and an interminable, untimely telephone call from Headquarters in Guernsey kept Captain Weiss at his desk until long after the hour when he usually had lunch. With some irritation, he sent word that his Adjutant and Medical Officer should begin without him. He thus missed overhearing a light-hearted conversation which, had he been there, would certainly have caused him to make immediate investigation. The Adjutant, a Lothario and newcomer to Armorel, remarked genially that things on the island could not be so dull as he had been led to believe owing to the reported presence of a beautiful young woman who waved to soldiers. The Medical Officer replied sourly that men of a certain temperament found anything in a skirt beautiful and there the subject was dropped. By the time Weiss arrived in Mess, the Adjutant was already on his rounds and the Medical Officer had gone down to the barracks to lance a corporal's suppurating finger. Weiss had lunch alone, last week's *Völkischer Beobachter* propped up against a flower vase. After lunch, he drank some lukewarm coffee, smoked a cigar and listened sleepily to a Bach concert relayed from Hamburg. It was half-past three when he returned to his office to take yet another telephone call from the Commandant at Guernsey.

It was the message that he had feared. He had hoped that the matter of Venus's removal to Germany would be delayed until after the birth of her calf so that he himself could claim to have been present on this most momentous occasion and, with his long experience of bovine breeding, made sure that all was well with her. He would have liked to have been the first to welcome her son. This was not to be. Dr. Goebbels' Propaganda Ministry had got hold of the Venus story and had decided to make the fullest use of it. A cargo boat was being sent to Armorel from Guernsey at six o'clock to take the animal to St. Peter Port. After rest and suitable refreshment, she would be flown by a specially prepared transport plane to an unnamed German airport where she would be welcomed by high Government officials and given the sort of reception only normally accorded to a film star. Her arrival would be broadcast to England on the 55-metre band and it would serve as a symbol of Germany's triumph over the pluto-democracies, her care for the future of pedigree breeding and her determination to . . .

"I know the rest," said Captain Weiss sadly. "Your orders will be carried out, *Herr Kommandant. Heil Hitler.*"

He put down the telephone with a sigh, rang the bell for his Adjutant. Sergeant Vogel answered the call. The Adjutant, he said, had not yet returned from his rounds. He would certainly be back in the next few minutes. He would see that he reported immediately on arrival.

Captain Weiss put on his cap and walked out of the Abbaye. He was very sorry that Venus was going and genuinely distressed at the use to which she was to be put. It seemed to him to be ethically wrong that an unsuspecting animal should be dragged into the black limelight of propaganda and made the subject of Dr. Goebbels' gleeful hysteria. There was nothing he could do about it. He was a soldier and orders were orders.

He approached Venus and stood looking at her affectionately. She was very heavy with calf. He ran his hand along her back, feeling her calving strings with sensitive fingers. It seemed to him that she was a little less tranquil than usual. She looked round her with bright eyes and shifted her feet. He pursed his lips. He pondered for a moment the advisability of telephoning to Guernsey and reporting that the animal was unfit to travel. With reluctance he dismissed the thought. To attempt in any way to impede the plans of Herr Doktor Goebbels would be to incur the displeasure of the Party and he was under no delusions as to the consequences of that. No, Venus must go and if she chose to calve in mid-air, that was just too bad. He scratched her head below her horns and talked to her softly in German. He gave her a final gentle slap on the flank and said, "*Auf wiedersehen, mein Liebchen, und gute Reise.*"

He walked back to the Abbaye. His Adjutant had returned and was waiting for him. Captain Weiss sat down at his desk and took off his cap.

"You sent for me, *Herr Kommandant*?"

"Yes, Müller. I have had orders from Guernsey that the cow Venus is to be taken there to-night and then flown to Germany. Please instruct Baptiste the cowman to take her to the harbour at half-past five. Her arrival in Germany is to be the subject of a triumphant broadcast to England. It is not for me to criticize the Propaganda Ministry but . . ." He shrugged and added, "I had hoped to keep her here until she had calved, but what can one do? Propaganda is greater than progeny."

Müller smiled cheerfully.

"You won't miss her so much, *Herr Kommandant*. After all, there is another Venus on the island."

"Another Venus. What do you mean?"

The Adjutant kissed his finger-tips with an air of gallantry.

"This is not a cow but a lady, a most beautiful lady. Young, strange and beautiful."

"A young and beautiful stranger in Armorel. Who is she?"

"That I have tried to find out but nobody knows. Every man in the working party saw her this morning."

Weiss said, frowning, "Why was I not informed of this?"

"I told the Medical Officer at lunch-time. But you were not there." He stopped and his hands flew to his mouth. He said in a low voice:

"*Mein Gott*."

"Well, what is it?" said Weiss sharply.

"*Herr Kommandant*, there is another thing. I wonder if . . . if . . ."

"If what? Speak."

"This morning, four, six of our soldiers were drinking coffee in the *Estaminet des Anges* when Jean, who is a member of the Court, came in. He was very drunk and he shouted at them that the war was over and that he had seen the sister of the Suzerain. Could it be possible that . . ."

Captain Weiss sprang to his feet.

"I am told nothing of these happenings. Why not?"

"*Herr Kommandant*, the soldiers paid little attention. The old man was very drunk and they thought—they thought he was raving. The Provost of Armorel came and took him away."

"Where is he now, this drunk man?"

"I don't know. The Provost took him away."

"He is to be found and brought to me, drunk or sober." He banged the bell on his desk and Sergeant Vogel came hurrying into the room.

"*Zum Befehl, Herr Kommandant.*"

"Sergeant Vogel, you will go at once to the *Estaminet des Anges* and seek the man Jean and bring him to me, no matter what his condition may be. You, Müller, you will instruct the N.C.O. and three men of the working party who actually saw this strange lady to report to me. I will talk to them separately, one after the other. You will also instruct those men who were in the *Estaminet des Anges* to stand by for questioning. I also wish to interview the Provost of Armorel *after* I have seen the N.C.O. and men of the working party. You understand?"

"I understand, *Herr Kommandant. Herr Kommandant,* do you think . . ."

"I think that you are a fool and that you may suffer harshly for your idiocy. Go to your duty."

Captain Weiss strode to the door and ran up the wide staircase of the Abbaye. He unlocked the door of Luke Fallaize's bedroom and marched inside and pulled the dust sheets off the dressing-table, on which was standing a large photograph in a plain silver frame. It was a photograph of a young woman in a white court dress and ostrich feathers in her hair. She carried a posy of flowers in her gloved hand and on her delicate sensitive face there was a look of pride. On the back was written: "For Luke from Nicola, June 1939." Captain Weiss stared at the photograph. Then he picked it up, walked back to his office grimly, and laid it face downwards on his desk.

"This is Corporal Kurt Schneider, *Herr Kommandant.* N.C.O. in charge of the working party this morning."

"Ah. Did you pass a young lady as you marched your men back to barracks?"

"Yes, sir."

"Was she known to you, this young lady?"

"No, sir."

"You have never seen her before in your life?"

"No, sir. Never."

Captain Weiss leaned forward intently.

"Would you know her again, corporal?"

"Yes, sir. I would know her again."

Captain Weiss picked up the photograph of Nicola and handed it to Corporal Schneider.

"Have you ever seen that lady before?"

Corporal Schneider glanced at the photograph. He said instantly:

"This is the young lady I saw this morning, sir. Yes. It is she."

"So." Captain Weiss raised his eyebrows. "You are sure of this?"

"I am certain, sir. She was not wearing a dress like in this photograph and she had no feathers in her hair. But I am quite certain."

"You are a dolt, Corporal Schneider. Do you think that a lady walks round a remote island dressed as if to meet the English King? Fall out and wait over there. Müller, bring in the next man."

The two men who followed recognized the photograph immediately and without hesitation as being that of the lady who had waved to them that morning. The third man was not so sure until Weiss covered the ostrich feathers with his hand. Then he, too, agreed with his comrades. Identification was complete. Captain Weiss said sternly:

"Why was the presence of this strange lady not instantly reported to the Adjutant?"

Corporal Schneider hesitated. He glanced at the Adjutant and at the floor, shuffling his feet.

"Answer me."

"Sir, with respect to the Adjutant, we thought that . . . that she must be a young lady brought over from Guernsey by the Adjutant. Sir, we . . . we imagined that it might be the *fiancée* of the Adjutant . . ."

"You have made yourself perfectly clear, Corporal," said Captain Weiss in frigid tones. "Do not leave this building and speak to nobody."

As the men trailed sheepishly out of the room, there was a dramatic interruption. Sergeant Vogel brushed past them and saluted. He said breathlessly, "*Herr Kommandant*, I have found the man Jean."

"Where is he? My instructions were that you should bring him here."

"It is impossible to move him. He is lying on a bed of straw in an outhouse of the *Estaminet des Anges*."

"Is he drunk?"

"No, he is not drunk, *Herr Kommandant.* He has a fearful wound on the back of the head."

Captain Weiss stood up, his chair went over with a crash. He rapped out his orders.

"All sentries will be issued with fifty rounds of ammunition, the cliff guards will be doubled and take up their posts at once. All guns will be manned. An orderly is to stand by to ring the general alarm on the church bell. At curfew, every house on the island will be searched and the woman Nicola Fallaize will be found and brought to my headquarters. The Medical Officer will examine the man Jean and report to me."

Unconsciously, his hand dropped to the butt of his Lueger automatic.

"I will now interview my friend the Provost of Armorel."

The noonday strength had gone from the sun. For the hundredth time, Nicola looked at her watch. She said shakily: "Well, I suppose I'd better get on with it."

Lionel Fallaize said in a low voice:

"I hate your doing this."

"I don't like it much myself."

"Nicola, darling Nicola, couldn't I go instead?"

"No. Nobody would be surprised if they saw me leading a cow about the place. But they'd expect you to be leading your pet python with scenes from the Garden of Eden painted on its skin."

"I haven't got a pet python. That was somebody else."

"Sorry. So it was. Lionel, I'm going now."

The wash of distemper had dried on Hyacinth's skin. Nicola led the painted travesty of Venus out of the yard and across the field opposite towards the sheltering gorse. She pegged her down in the lower pasture, in distant sight of the windows of the Abbaye. Then she walked back through the gorse and into the top pasture.

In the mellow sunshine the only sound was that of Venus tugging grass. Nicola walked towards her. Venus looked up. It was immediately apparent to her that she was in some discomfort. She moved restlessly and twitched her ears. Nicola loosened the steel peg with her heel, drew it out of the soft earth and said in a pleading voice:

"Come on, Venus—and for the Lord's sake, come quickly."

She gave a tug at the rope.

With a reproachful air at these continued interruptions, Venus allowed herself to be led to the top road.

The greatest danger of all lay before Nicola.

To reach Lionel's house, she had to pass directly in front of the windows of the Abbaye.

Captain Weiss sat at his desk, his back to the window. The Provost of Armorel stood before him.

"You sent for me, *Monsieur le Commandant*."

"Yes, I did. There are two matters concerning which I require a full and immediate explanation. A stranger, a young lady, was seen in Armorel this morning. Who and where is this lady?"

The Provost's lined face remained impassive but his hands slowly clenched.

"*Monsieur le Commandant* must be mistaken."

"That is all you have to say?"

"That is all."

"So be it. I now come to the second matter. The man Jean, a member of your Court, was led by you from the *Estaminet des Anges*. He has since been found, wounded, unconscious—and speechless. Why, *Monsieur le Provost*, was it necessary to silence his tongue?"

"I . . . I have no explanation to offer."

"But I have." Captain Weiss's normally friendly voice was sharp with menace. "The strange lady in Armorel is Miss Nicola Fallaize, sister of the absent

Suzerain. She has landed—or been landed—secretly on the island. It is possible that she has not come alone." He picked up the photograph. "Is this or is this not Miss Nicola Fallaize?"

"It is Miss Nicola, monsieur."

"It is also the lady who walks the roads of Armorel. She was seen and recognized by Jean who, poor drunken fool, blurted out the news. That is why he was led away by you and brutally attacked. If he should die, you and those associated with you will be charged with murder and executed."

The telephone bell rang. Captain Weiss snatched the receiver.

"Who? Mrs. Guilleaume. You wish to report what? That one of your cows has been stolen." He said with heavy sarcasm, "Mrs. Guilleaume, is it your wish that I, the Commandant of Armorel, should search the island for a missing cow? Possibly you would like me to divert the garrison from their duties so that every field may be combed for your lost treasure. Do not waste my time with trivialities. Good night, Mrs. Guilleaume." He banged down the receiver. "Now, *Monsieur le Provost*, the answer to my questions please. Where is Miss Nicola Fallaize? What is her purpose on the island of Armorel, and did she come alone?"

The Provost was looking straight over Captain Weiss's shoulder. Before his eyes, he saw Nicola. She was bare-headed and she walked the top road leading the ponderous Venus behind her. By no flicker of the eyelid did he indicate what was in his startled vision. Only when Nicola and Venus had passed from his sight did he speak.

"I cannot answer your questions, monsieur."

"Listen to me. The island is ringed with sentries. She has no chance of getting away. Now will you speak?"

Who would counsel the islanders now? To whose voice would they listen in their doubts and their fears? The autumn would come and the winter and the loop of steel would be tightened. There would be no Suzerain and no Provost and only God could foretell what would happen to the little community whom he loved and longed to protect. Who would get up in the hard mornings and collect the eggs and feed the hens, who would thread the needles for Marie, who would stoke the stove on the winter mornings to come? The Provost of Armorel sighed. He said, deliberately speaking the patois of the island:

"I have nothing to tell you."

"Very well. You are under arrest. You are forbidden to leave the Abbaye."

"As *Monsieur le Commandant says.*"

It seemed to Nicola that she had been walking for hours and hours by the time she reached Lionel's back-yard and shut the door behind Venus's lazily swinging tail. She said weakly:

"Here's the lady. I've never known before what a coward I am. I don't . . . think Venus is terribly well and I . . . do . . . think I'm going to be sick."

CHAPTER EIGHTEEN

DROOPING HYACINTH

At half-past five Baptiste left his cottage. The Provost had told him what to do and he proposed to do it without question. His face was impassive as he walked the familiar path by the side of the maize field, by the golden oats ready for harvesting, past the gap in the wire netting which he had so often promised himself to mend. He entered the lower meadow. A cow was grazing in the hollow where the greedy gorse menaced the grass perpetually. Baptiste came up to her and stopped. He gazed at her with his clear fisherman's eyes and a strange thing happened. Baptiste laughed. The innumerable tiny lines in the skin of his face dissolved and from his mouth came a rumbling, deep-throated chuckle. Oh yes. Mr. Lionel had certainly done his work well. Now he would lead this . . . this creature to the harbour and the Germans would take her away and never know how they had been tricked . . . *s'il plaît au Seigneur.*

Still chuckling, he led the patient, painted Hyacinth across the field to the high road and to the *Colline des Mouettes.*

There seemed to be an unusual activity on the island. He passed groups of German soldiers who were marching purposefully and he noticed that they were armed. Their faces were set and none of them shouted a cheerful greeting or waved their hands. They looked like soldiers going into battle. Perhaps it was as well that nobody had time to stop and pass the time of day—for the creature he led could certainly not bear any close examination. . . . Baptiste walked on. At Garrison Headquarters, a sentry, grim-faced and unsmiling, barred his way. Baptiste stopped. Hyacinth moved to the side of the road and began to graze on the grass verge.

"Where are you going?"

"I am instructed to take this cow to the harbour."

"Who gave the order?"

"It is the order of the Commandant. I had my instructions from the Provost."

"So." The sentry shifted his Lueger from his right hand to his left. "Why is the cow to go to the harbour?"

Baptiste looked at the sentry with his clear blue eyes.

"I am not one to question instructions, monsieur." There was dignity and reproof in his voice. "I obey. This cow is Venus de l'Abbaye and she is going to Germany."

"*Ach ja.* I have heard something of this." He stepped to one side. "You may pass."

"Thank you, monsieur." Baptiste gave a tug at Hyacinth's head-rope. He said in his rumbling voice, "Come, Venus."

Now he had lied to the Germans and punishment

would follow. So be it. He was an old man and he had lived his life. It had been a full life and a tranquil one. It might even be that he would soon lie in the churchyard under the sound of the bell. Well, if that was going to happen, it would happen . . . *s'il plaît au Seigneur*. He said again deliberately:

"Come, Venus."

Man and beast slowly turned the corner of the stony road that led to the harbour.

Captain Weiss glanced at his watch and at the Adjutant. He said curtly:

"I am going to the harbour to make sure that Venus gets aboard safely. Those dolts of fishermen know nothing of how to handle cattle and they could easily break her leg. I shall be back in twenty minutes."

"Very good, *Herr Kommandant*."

Weiss banged the gate of the Abbaye behind him and took the road to the *Colline des Mouettes*. At Garrison Headquarters, the watchful sentry leapt to attention.

"*Zum Befehl, Herr Kommandant*."

"Have you anything to report?"

"Yes, *Herr Kommandant*. I permitted a man to take the cow Venus to the harbour. He said that it was your order."

"It was indeed by my order. No one else is permitted to pass. See to it."

"*Zum Befehl, Herr Kommandant*."

Captain Weiss acknowledged the clicked heels with an absent-minded salute; he strode on. As he came to the bend in the serpentine road that briefly overlooked the harbour, he saw far below him that the promised cargo boat had already arrived from Guernsey and was lying alongside. Her crew had hoisted a gangway and, tiny in the distance, he saw a cow being led across the cobbled quay to its head. He saw her put a tentative hoof on it and back away, as if unwilling to trust her weight to this fragile link between shore and ship. Captain Weiss frowned. He was the one, the only one, who knew how to coax Venus. He hurried, half-running, down the steep hill and came breathlessly upon the quay. In that brief space of time, the cow had evidently been reassured and had changed her mind for she was more than half-way down the gangway. Baptiste the cowman was at her head and he was drawing her inch by inch towards the deck. He had spread sacking on the gangway's corrugations and Weiss had time to approve in another what he would have done himself. All was well with her. But the light sou'-wester that had blown all day was increasing in strength, packing the young flood tide into the harbour, and the vessel rocked uneasily on the swell. It seemed to Weiss that the cow suddenly sensed danger, for she threw up her head and backed, driving her bony rump against the gangway rail. The rusty iron crumpled under the thrust and buckled outwards. Captain Weiss shouted:

"Stop. Baptiste, stay by her head. I will come."

Baptiste looked up, saw the Commandant of Armorel. A look of horror stamped itself on the old man's face and he struggled to speak. His words came huskily:

"It is all right, monsieur. *Tout va bien.* Please do not come."

The cow's body was wedged diagonally across the gangway and she heaved convulsively as she saw the surging water below. Weiss ran to the gangway. Baptiste said again in a pleading voice:

"Please do not come, monsieur. *Je vous en prie. Tout va bien.*"

"Do you want her to fall into the sea, you fool? Move her head to the right . . . easily now. Easily."

"Monsieur . . ."

Captain Weiss walked quietly and on tiptoe down the gangway. He put his hand on the cow's hip-bone and pressed firmly. Under his strong, steady pressure her body moved.

"Bring her head more to the right. Excellent. Now I think she will be all right."

He took his hand away, conscious of a strange stickiness. He glanced at his palm and saw to his astonishment that it was covered with brown pigment. He looked sharply at the cow and at his hand. He took a swift step forward and ran his other hand down her trembling, sweating flank. He stared at his fingers. A few hairs clung to the paint, moist and warm from the heat and secretions of the animal's body. He darted up the gangway and along the quay to where he could see her sideways. He only needed one glance to confirm the fearful suspicion that had come to him in the last thirty seconds. He jerked his Lueger from its holster and stood with his jack-booted feet menacingly astride.

"Stop. Take that animal ashore."

Baptiste looked at him, his old face a mask.

"*Mais, monsieur* . . ."

"Take that animal ashore, I say. So you think to make a fool of me and of Germany, do you? By God, you will learn."

"*Mais, monsieur* . . ."

"Do as I say." He laughed but there was no humour in his laughter. "So the island of Armorel stages a pantomime, does it. We will see who can put on the best display. That painted creature is not Venus." His voice rose to a furious, strangled shout. "She is not Venus, she is not Venus, she is not Venus."

At long last, dusk began to dim the fields of Armorel. The smell of gorse and wood-smoke and thyme laced the air and there was a great chattering of magpies, harsh as machinery against the evening singing of larks and wrens and the fluting of blackbirds. The wind was getting up and Valentine Morland, lying in a clump of bracken near the top of the road that became the path to the *Pointe de Joie*, looked uneasily at the gusty trees. As silently as a Red Indian, Alexander Forbes wormed his way through the bracken and rested on his elbows beside him.

"Hullo, Alec."

"Hullo, Mr. Valentine." He smiled his slow smile. "There's a terrible lot of anxiety about. It's like the day I put up my peregrine tiercel over the snipe bog."

"What's happened?"

"I don't know much. But they're ringing the island with sentries and the Provost went to the Abbaye hours ago. He hasn't come out yet, and by the way, I've cut the telephone lines from the *Pointe de Joie*. When's Miss Nicola coming?"

"Soon now, when it gets a bit darker. I'm worried about her, Alec."

"I know you are, Mr. Valentine."

"I let her do too much."

"It was the only way. We didn't know when we landed what we were up against. She did. She's a fine girl, Mr. Valentine."

"If they caught her, what would they do to her?"

Alexander Forbes said soothingly:

"You don't want to start thinking about things like that." He licked his finger and held it up. "Wind's coming from the south-west and it's rising. There'll be quite a tide to take us out." There was a long silence. Alec said with quiet emphasis:

"I said 'to take us out', Mr. Valentine."

"I heard you. I wish she'd come."

"What will you do if she doesn't come?"

"Go back and look for her. I'm not going without her."

"No. Of course not. We couldn't do that."

"We?"

"Yes. 'We.' " He rolled over on his back and gazed

up into the dimness of the sky. He said after a long while, "She's a fine girl. I didn't think they made them that way nowadays."

"Neither did I. But they do."

The two men were silent as a deeper darkness came over the woods of Armorel and the birds, their songs sung, took to the windy trees.

Captain Weiss walked into his office and sat down. He kept on his peaked cap. He rapped out his orders.

"The man Baptiste is to be held in close arrest. All sentries are to remain at the alert and all movement on the island—either of man or beast—is to be stopped forthwith. Has the Medical Officer reported on the condition of the man Jean?"

"Yes, *Herr Kommandant.* He continues to breathe but it will be some hours before he regains consciousness. It is considered that he will live."

"In some hours it will be dark. Warn the Commander of the E-boat *Lübeck* to be ready to put to sea at a moment's notice for action."

"*Zum Befehl, Herr Kommandant.*"

"I have decided to handle this little affair myself. No word of it is to reach German Headquarters in Guernsey until it is over, when my report will, I think, make most interesting reading. I will now see the Provost."

"*Zum Befehl, Herr Kommandant.*"

It was strange indeed to be held prisoner within the walls of a house that he knew and loved and the Provost of Armorel kept looking around the room with bewildered eyes. When the Adjutant again summoned him to Captain Weiss, he went slowly and with a heavy step. Captain Weiss said evenly:

"Some half an hour ago, I asked you to tell me the whereabouts of Miss Nicola Fallaize. You refused to speak. I now ask you to tell me the whereabouts of the pedigree cow, Venus de l'Abbaye."

The Provost's heart sank. So all had been in vain . . . but they had not yet found her. The hours were running out as the tide was coming in. Time and darkness were the friends of his friends and every minute of freedom helped. The Provost looked at the floor and at the cracks in the floor. He said at last:

"How should I know? Surely, monsieur, the cow Venus is on her way to Germany. That was monsieur's order. I have been held prisoner, so I have no means of knowing if that order has been obeyed. But Baptiste had his orders. He had his orders from me, *Monsieur le Commandant.*"

"I am glad that you admit so much. Your friend and ally Baptiste sought to carry out your instructions. He tried to insult the Führer and the Reich by sending a half-bred creature painted like a prostitute to Germany. But he failed. Your little pantomime is over, *Monsieur le Provost,* and the curtain is down. Now it is our turn. Had your friend Baptiste been worth a bullet, his body would already be feeding the cormorants. As it is, he will—if he is lucky—spend the few remaining years of his life *at your side* in a German Concentration

Camp. You will learn what it means to insult the Führer. . . ."

The Provost said mildly:

"Hyacinth is a good cow. It is true that she has not got the breeding of Venus but she was sired by Majestic White and her dam was Lady White of les Pellys de Bas. There is Maple Lodge blood on both sides and——"

"Silence. I have no wish to discuss the blood-lines of a painted harridan. Where is Venus de l'Abbaye?"

The Provost shrugged. In the silence that followed the steady tick-tock, tick-tock, tick-tock of the grandfather clock in the hall was clear. Darkness was falling, the wind was rising and the tide on the flood. His friends were still free. . . .

"There have been many curious happenings on this island in the last few hours, *Monsieur le Provost*. Let me enumerate them. Miss Nicola Fallaize, sister of the absent Suzerain, honours the island with her presence. The drunken fool Jean shouts the news in his cups and is silenced—by your order. The pedigree cow Venus vanishes—and an attempt is made to substitute an inferior animal painted to resemble her markings. I wonder who the clever artist could be. I wonder if a certain symbolist and pacifist called Mr. Lionel Fallaize can have forsaken canvas for . . . cow hide."

The Provost said nothing. He was conscious all the time that the tide was surging towards the rocks of the *Pointe de Joie* bearing the hopes of salvation on every incoming wave. . . .

"I wonder what the connection is between these

seemingly unrelated events. A few more hours will show. The stage is set for the next act—or shall I say 'the last act'?—of your island comedy. I fear it may be tragic—for Armorel. You will continue to remain at the Abbaye under escort of the Adjutant. If at any moment you wish to have a conversation with me, I shall be at your disposal. *Au revoir, Monsieur le Provost.*"

"*Au revoir, Monsieur le Commandant.*"

Lionel Fallaize got up and groped his way across the dim studio, peered through the tightly drawn curtains.

"What's it like?"

"It'll soon be dark." He chuckled. "I think this is an occasion for candle-light." He was gay and buoyant for there was a well of joy within him. As he crossed the room, feeling his way, he bumped into an unfamiliar object and said, "I'm sorry, madam. My fault entirely." He found a silver candle-stick on the book-case, struck a match. The tiny yellow spear tip of flame illuminated a fantastic scene. Nicola sat in a rickety armchair, blinking in the light. The half-finished picture stood on its easel; but the calm gaze of the Godhead and the grin of the ape were fixed on a living cow, her head-rope looped round the leg of an upright piano, her bulging body between the book-case and the writing-desk.

"Shall I play to her? I read somewhere cows have a highly developed taste in music." He opened the piano and began to sing softly to a rippling tune:

Venus s'est assise
Tra- la- la.
A l'ombre d'un rocher
A son plaisir écoute
Tra- la- la.
Les mariniers chanter
Tra- la- la! Tra- la- la.

He stopped singing but his fingers, not only sensitive but steady and strong, took up the melody lightly and played it again. He said to her, looking at the keyboard:

"What's the chap like, the one you call Valentine?"

Nicola frowned. In the last hours, hardly a thought of Valentine had crossed her mind. He was a person whom she had met and known briefly—years ago. Now she realized with a sense of surprise that this unremembered man was on the island of Armorel, sharing her danger, wanting to protect her with his strength. It was with an effort that she found words to describe him.

"He's a nice person. He's gentle and he gives one a great sense of security."

"Is he in love with you?"

"In love with me?" She hesitated. "That's an odd question, Lionel."

He turned his head and smiled, the flashing, imperious smile of the dominant schoolboy.

"Nicky—tell."

"I don't know. I think he may think he is."

"Oh. And you, my darling? What about you?"

"Well, what about me?"

He went on playing but the melody had changed. Now it was "Greensleeves" and he sang in a soft, almost ragging voice:

> "*For I have loved you well and long*
> *Delighting in your companee. . . .*"

She stood up and walked over to him and stood behind him and slid her arms around his neck so that her left hand lay over his heart.

"You're an awful ass, Lionel."

"And you're a lovely girl. I would think hardly of anyone who, knowing you, didn't love you. But I'm here and you're there, full of zest and health. . . . Tell, Nicky. What about you?"

It was hard to find words.

"I don't know if you will understand this because I don't understand it myself. I accept it as one accepts sunrise and sunset and . . . and God. In the last year since I left Armorel, I have been taken out to parties and to dine and things by lots of men, people whom I've liked. Valentine's one of them. And then there always comes a moment when I look at them and then, suddenly, I know that they're not you. It's very disappointing in a way . . . but not really. Their hair isn't like yours and their hands are different and they don't walk in the way that you walk and then they've never pulled a mackerel hook out of my bloomers in a northeaster and you have. It's a great shock to a girl because one moment they're fun to be with and the next moment they simply don't exist. That's what you've done to me, Lionel. That's what you'll always do to me." She stopped, abashed at a phrase that came readily. She said it. "You are bone of my bone and flesh of my flesh." She shut her eyes. She took fright and darted away like a deer. "But don't think for one instant that I don't like Valentine because I do. And if you weren't here, I could like him a lot more."

He swung round on the piano stool and stood up, shutting the keyboard with a great bang. Venus threw her head and backed away. He said, his eyes alight:

"Sorry, Venus. I forgot about you. Nicola, I don't know what's going to happen, but we're all in danger. You know that."

"Yes, I know that. I'm not a brave person but at the moment I don't care a damn. Sorry. That's A.T.S. language."

"I want to take you in my arms and to kiss your mouth."

"You never have and, well . . . here I am."

Venus shifted her feet and lowed disconsolately. The sound of marching boots went past the curtained window, died away.

"How nice your hair smells."

"It's not me. It's Chanel Number Five. Pre-war. I'm a conventional girl, I am."

"Conventional! That's why you come to me in the darkest days of the war as if you were going to a ball. But this isn't a dance." He looked around him with a sense of wonder. He said slowly, "Candle-light, Chanel and cow-dung. . . ."

"Yes. I'm afraid Venus isn't house-trained. Lionel, I love it when you kiss me. I'm me for the first time in my life."

Her spine was pliant. It was a full minute before she heard a soft repeated tapping on the window-pane. She broke away from him and caught his fingers in a fierce grip.

"Listen!"

They stood tense. The tapping was insistent. Lionel said in a low voice:

"Wait. I'll go."

He tiptoed to the door. Nicola stood by Venus, her knees trembling and her heart beating like a hammer under her breast. She heard the sound of whispering and then the door opened quietly. Lionel said, smiling:

"It's all right, darling. A friend has come to call."

The little boy Georges slipped into the room. He said to her breathlessly:

"Miss Nicola, I knew you were here, you and Venus. Your friend Mr. Valentine is taking me to England with you. But there is danger now, great danger."

"What has happened?"

"The Germans are searching every house on the island for you and for Venus." He grinned and quoted an old island proverb. "*Changement d'herbage est bon pour les jeunes veaux!* Miss Nicola, you must go."

"But you, Georges, what will you do?"

"Sergeant Vogel is a fool. He is in charge of the

search party. I will tell him that I have seen you by the *Baie de l'Ondine* and he will go there to search. At the top of the path to the *Pointe de Joie*, there is a little shed. There you will be quite safe and there I will come to you. Monsieur Valentine and your other friend are waiting by the bend of the road. But you must go now."

"I will. Georges, be very careful."

"Sergeant Vogel, I say, is a fool. I will send him to the *Baie de l'Ondine. Au revoir, Mademoiselle Nicola.*"

"*Au revoir, Georges.* Come back very soon."

The little boy was gone. Deliberately Lionel Fallaize began to untie the knot of the rope that tethered Venus to the leg of the piano. He said easily:

"I'll just come and see you off."

"But you're coming too and you haven't packed or anything."

He said, his back to her:

"I can easily buy a toothbrush when I get there. He who travels light, travels fastest. You take the mushrooms, Nicky, and I'll take the lady. Before we go, I want to tell you that I love you very much. That's all. Whoa up, Venus. . . ."

CHAPTER NINETEEN

GEORGES

IN this moment of emergency, Lionel Fallaize seemed to acquire a new stature. He was calm and practical and he took easy command. He drew Venus to the door of the studio and through the kitchen and into the backyard. He looked up at the sky and frowned. The wind was now blowing in almost continuous gusts and ragged wisps of dark cloud sailed across the stars from the south-west. The night air was cool and sweet in his lungs.

"Nicky, darling, can you hold the gate open? I'll take her through and then you can go on ahead and keep in the shadow of the hedges. How are we for time?"

"High tide's at sixteen past ten."

"That gives us about half an hour. We should just about make it—provided nothing happens to . . . er . . . delay us *en route*. Where are your boy-friends?"

"In the bracken by the twist of the road."

"You'd better slip ahead and warn them that Venus and I are on the way. In this light they might think I was Sergeant Vogel and take what they considered to be appropriate action." He chuckled. "I am the apostle of non-violence, British or German. If anything happens, hoot like an owl."

"But I don't know how to hoot like an owl."

"They should have taught you before you left London. Hooting like an owl is *de rigueur* on this sort of expedition. We'd better get moving."

He gave a gentle tug at the head-rope. Venus followed him very slowly. After a few yards she stopped and breathed deeply. It was evident that she was in some distress, but she recovered and took up her obedient, uneasy progress. Nicola walked ahead on tiptoe. She reached the turn of the road and the fringe of the bracken. Standing in the darkness she whispered shakily:

"Valentine."

He rose and came to her and took both her hands. He said solemnly:

"Thank God you've come."

She smiled, her face white in the gloom.

"Surely you didn't think I'd lost my way." She freed her hands gently. "Is Alec all right?"

"Here I am, Miss Nicola. I'm fine."

"Things are not good. My cousin Lionel is bringing Venus, but . . . but I don't think the walk is doing her any good. He'll be here in a moment. And the Germans know something's up. All the houses on the island are being searched. They know I'm here. They've got extra guards on the cliffs. Valentine, I . . . I think we're in for a bad night."

"What rot you talk. Alec and I can deal with the

sentries and they can search the houses till they're blue in the face because we're all out of doors. All of us. Remember the falling star, Nicola?"

"That was a million years ago. One more thing. Georges, the little boy Georges, is going to tell Vogel that he's seen me at the far end of the island, by the *Baie de l'Ondine*. Then he's going to join us here. You do think he'll be all right, don't you?"

"Sergeant Vogel or Georges?"

"Georges."

"Of course he will. It would take a charge of high explosives to damage that infant. Have you still got your mushrooms?"

"Yes, but they're a bit squashed."

"We'll have to have them in a *purée*."

There was the sound of a hoof on a stone and in the gusty gloom Lionel Fallaize led Venus very slowly up to the group. Nicola said, "This is my cousin Lionel, who paints pictures—and cows. This is Valentine Morland, and the desperado with the revolver is Alec Forbes. How's Venus, Lionel?"

"The lady has her health. But only just. I rather think we are going to be confronted by another problem—or should I say an extra passenger—at any moment."

Alexander Forbes carefully shielded the light of his torch with his hand, flashed it at Venus. The narrow beam of light travelled over her full belly and her twitching flank. Alec said quickly:

"Is there any shelter near?"

"Yes. There's a shed in about a hundred yards."

"We'd better get her there at once."

There was a fine web of rain in the wind and the taste of it was salt on Nicola's lips.

"Alec . . . is it . . .?"

"Yes it is, Miss Nicola." His voice was very gentle. "We can go no further. Venus is just going to have her calf."

Valentine said nothing. He peered at his watch and saw the second-hand nibbling away steadily at the precious minutes. He laid his hand soothingly on Venus's straight spine. He wished passionately that Alec and he had come alone.

The German patrol, led by Sergeant Vogel, marched along the road that led to the Provost's cottage. As he neared the hen-houses he noticed a little figure slip through a gap in the hedge and run towards the cottage. His eyes narrowed but he did not speak. He halted his men at the door and knocked loudly. The Provost's wife opened. He said to her:

"Good evening. I have orders to search the house."

She drew back, her hand to her breast. The German soldiers filed past her, their heavy boots making a great clatter. Sergeant Vogel walked into the living-room. Georges sat on a stool by the fireplace. As Sergeant Vogel came into the room he glanced up superciliously and returned to his book. Vogel's face contorted itself into what was meant to be a genial smile.

"Well, my little boy, and how long have you been sitting there?"

"Since curfew."

The smile faded. "Oh, all the time. That is interesting."

"No. Not all the time."

"So! And where have you been?"

"Down the garden."

"Down the . . ." Into his face came a look of understanding. "You have only been down the garden?"

"Where do you think I go? To the public lavatory by the *Havre des Mouettes*? I have no time to waste—like some people."

"What do you mean?"

Georges shut his book. He said loftily:

"I have no time to waste—like you. Here you are looking for a lady. But she is not here. Therefore I say that you are wasting your time."

Sergeant Vogel's eyes were suddenly alert. He said softly, "How do you know, little one, that we are looking for a lady?"

Georges shifted his feet uneasily and looked away. "I know many things."

"Of course you do. Then you can tell me where the lady is to be found?"

"Yes. The lady is by the *Baie de l'Ondine*."

"You are a very clever little boy," he said in coaxing tones. "Will you take me to this lady?"

"Me? No. I . . . I . . . have to have supper. But if you go to the *Baie de l'Ondine* you will find Miss Nico——" He stopped and went on lamely, "You will find the lady. I don't know her name."

The sitting-room door opened and a soldier looked in. He said rapidly in German:

"Sergeant, would you please come. We have found something."

Sergeant Vogel stood up. He gave Georges a playful cuff on the shoulder.

"You will stay until I come back. You will not go —down the garden again."

"I am a boy—not a little dog running round the tree-trunks."

"Good. Then you stay until I return."

Sergeant Vogel followed the soldier into the tiny back bedroom where Georges slept. On the bed was a bundle tied with string. Vogel picked it up and turned it over in his hand. Then, very carefully, he undid the string. Wrapped up in a clean shirt and a pair of much mended trousers was a thick cheese sandwich and a toy revolver. Sergeant Vogel stared at these objects, his eyes blinking rapidly. He tied up the bundle again and put it under the pillow where the soldier had found it. He said softly in German to the soldier:

"We will leave here now—and start for the *Baie de l'Ondine*. I will break off and return here quietly. I think our little friend may soon leave this house again and lead me to the lady we seek. Come."

Sergeant Vogel walked back to the hall. The Provost's wife said to him anxiously:

"Monsieur, can you please tell me where my husband is? He has not returned."

"Ach, your husband!" He chuckled. "Your husband must learn not to play games with the German Army. Have no fears, madame. Your husband is in very good hands. Oh, yes. Very good. And now I wish you good night. And to the little boy as well—good night."

In what was intended to be a crushing silence, Georges opened his book.

The patrol marched noisily into the gloom. When the sound of their marching had died away, Georges grinned. He went into his bedroom and picked up the bundle. He untied it, tucked the toy revolver in his belt and tied it up again. He slid out through the back door and began to trot towards the road that led to the *Pointe de Joie*. He was very proud of his cleverness and very happy—and blissfully unaware that Sergeant Vogel, his ten-shot Lueger in his hand, was following silently at his heels.

The interior of the shed was pitch dark and the wind whistled through the cracks in the wall. It took Valentine and Alec a full ten minutes before they led Venus through a door that hung drunkenly on one hinge. Nicola had gone ahead and was waiting for them. She said anxiously: "Is she still all right?"

"Yes."

"Lionel's gone back to his home to get some candles."

"Fine."

He came back. He had been running and he was breathing hard. He said:

"Sorry I was so long. But I had to lie in a ditch while a patrol passed. They'd been to my house. Anyone got a match?"

"Here you are."

The flickering flame of the candle illuminated every corner of the shed. Cobwebs were looped round the dusty rafters and a rusty length of chain hung down from the main beam. There was a mouldering pile of sacking by the gaping window and from it a fat brown rat peered at them and then scuttled across the uneven floor and squeezed itself under the door with a wriggle of its scaly tail. Nicola gave a gasp of horror and took a quick, instinctive step towards Lionel. He slipped his arm around her shoulders and held her strongly.

"All right, Nicky. It's gone."

"I know. But it was beastly."

Lionel looked around the shed. He said, smiling at Valentine, "It's not exactly Queen Charlotte's, is it, Morland?"

"I've known more elegant maternity hospitals."

"It's odd how impotent one becomes in the presence of the ancient verities. No man can arrest or accelerate the process of maternity; no one can stem the flow of the tide."

Valentine looked at Lionel with curiosity. He saw a lean, dark face and ruffled untidy hair. The eyes were very bright, the mouth clean-cut and smiling. So this was Nicola's cousin Lionel. This was the man about whom she had spoken with reluctance, a reluctance which he had utterly misunderstood. Now all was clear to him. This was the man who had grown up from the boy with whom she used to sail the tides of Armorel. This was the painter and the pacifist. Yet it was to the pacifist that she turned in a moment of horror and disgust and the arm that held her and gave her comfort was his arm. Superficially they were not alike, because she was fair and he was dark. But there *was* a likeness, an indefinable twinship about them that saddened his heart. He remembered a phrase he had once used and the circumstances in which he had used it. Clear-cut and sharp as an etching, he saw himself and Nicola sitting together in a London restaurant and he seemed to hear his own voice speak. He had said something about "the blood of Kings". The blood of Kings! The light-hearted words had referred then to a bottle of Burgundy. Now, strangely, they seemed to describe a hidden quality in two people, in Nicola and Lionel Fallaize. Why should he be conscious of a sense of intrusion in the presence of a stranger and of a girl whom he thought to have known so well? The flame of the candle flickered in the wind and he smiled at Nicola but not with his eyes.

"I hope you've brought a mushroom for your cousin, Nicola."

She said softly but with great warmth:

"Of course I have."

A shadow slid across the door as Georges came into the shed and put his bundle down. He walked straight to Nicola.

"I did what I said I would do. I have sent Sergeant

Vogel to the *Baie de l'Ondine.* Oh, but he is such a fool." He looked around, his eyes bright with pride. "Is this your friend, Mr. Valentine?"

"Yes, Georges. This is my friend. His name is Alec."

Georges solemnly put out his tiny hand.

"*Bonsoir, Monsieur Alec. Je m'appelle Georges.*"

"I'm afraid I can't speak French, Georges." He clasped the small hand in his strong, sunburned fingers. "But I'm very happy to meet you."

"And me too. Good evening, Mr. Lionel. Are you coming to England with us to fight the Germans?"

A voice, harsh as it was triumphant, rasped from the door of the shed.

"No, Herr Fallaize is not going to England. None of you is going to England. Back to the wall and put your hands up. *Schnell, Schnell* . . . or I shoot."

Trawler Langley was by the wheel of the M.T.B. as she passed *Petit Pigeon* at six knots, her bows dipping to the last of the flood tide. It had been an uneventful journey so far but the return trip promised to be something quite different for the wind was up and the seas were making. As the M.T.B. rounded *Petit Pigeon,* he saw in the half-light the great dark mass of the *Pointe de Joie* and, to the west, the twenty-five-foot channel of leaping sea that was so aptly called the *Couloir du Diable.* The Devil's Passage. Trawler measured it with his eye and grinned. Uncle George certainly knew what he was at. He spoke to the M.T.B. Commander and the helmsman swung the craft's bows toward the *Pointe*:

"She'll come in by herself now, sir," said Trawler.

The officer gave an order into the speaking-tube.

"Cut engines."

The grumble and bubble of the underwater exhaust died away. The Commander cupped his hands to his mouth and called softly.

"Stand by to let go forward. Keep the lead line going."

The only sound was the wind and the wet hiss and splash of the sea as the tide carried the M.T.B. rocking inshore and the low chant of the rating, reporting depth of water.

". . . and a half, three . . . by the mark, three . . . and a half, two . . . by the mark, two . . . and a half, one . . ."

"Let go."

The anchor slid almost soundlessly into the sea. Trawler Langley, shoulder-deep in water, waded ashore. He stood on the shelving beach and called softly: "Ahoy, ahoy. Major Morland, ahoy."

Over the whole island of Armorel brooded a vast stillness—made the more profound by the flurry of the wind.

CHAPTER TWENTY

DARK NURSERY

SERGEANT VOGEL leaned against the broken door of the shed and chuckled.

"So I find everything at once. A missing cow, a missing artist and Miss Nicola Fallaize. Also a little boy who thought he was very clever, and two strange gentlemen. Will you not introduce me to your friends, Herr Fallaize?"

" 'Mr.' Fallaize, please. Nicky, I told you you should have hooted like an owl."

"But I don't know how."

"Silence. You will all turn round and look to the wall." Vogel waved the barrel of his Lueger threateningly. "Turn round, all of you."

There was nothing Valentine could do—yet. With his hands above his head he turned slowly. Sergeant Vogel took his revolver and Alec's, threw them on the ground outside the door. At the sight of the toy pistol in Georges' belt he gave a great guffaw. He backed to the door again and cuddled his Lueger into the crook of his arm.

"You may now all turn again and face me. To the clever little boy who led me to you, I leave his pistol. We will have a nice conversation. Herr Fallaize."

"I have asked you, *ad nauseam*, to call me 'Mr.' Fallaize, Vogel."

"Good. From now until you and your friends are shot, I will call you 'Mr.'" He said craftily, "I suppose you wish that I should march you all to German Headquarters so that you could run away in the darkness. No, I do not do that. Here we wait until the soldiers come."

"May Miss Fallaize and Georges put their hands down?"

"No."

"I understand." Valentine's voice was like ice. "It is instructive to see that an armed N.C.O. in the German Army is afraid of an unarmed woman and of a little boy with a toy pistol."

Sergeant Vogel looked at him steadily. Under Valentine's contemptuous gaze he flushed. He said grudgingly:

"The woman and the boy may put their hands down. You—and you—and Mr. Fallaize will keep them up. Nobody is to move. If any of you moves, I shoot."

Lionel said musingly:

"I wonder if you'll get promotion for this, Vogel. I confess to a certain difficulty in visualizing you as an officer."

"Silence! We wait."

Valentine glanced upwards at the watch on his wrist. The second-hand was nibbling, nibbling, nibbling away . . . as the acid was nibbling away at the fuses that he had buried under the sands of the *Baie de l'Ondine*. . . .

The whimpering of the wind had increased and the door swung on its one rusted hinge. There was a low, plaintive sound from Venus. Nicola took a step forward.

"Stay where you are." Vogel scowled. "What is the matter with the cow?"

"Her calf is arriving." Nicola bit her lip and whispered, "Venus." She took another step forward. Vogel swung the barrel of his Lueger towards her. He half-shouted: "I say to you, get back to the wall."

"But she needs help."

"Get back."

"I will not get back," she said steadily. "I am going to Venus."

She walked deliberately across the uneven floor. She said softly, "It's all right, Venus. You are among friends. . . ."

In the Officers' Mess, Captain Hans Weiss sat in an armchair, a half-smoked cigar between his teeth. His Adjutant Müller was playing the piano very softly, the notes of "Frasquita" falling like snowflakes. Captain Weiss hardly heard the music. He said:

"It is nearly half-past ten. No news yet of the search party?"

"No news yet, *Herr Kommandant*."

"Strange, strange." He frowned. "You know what I believe, Müller?"

The Adjutant shut the piano quietly.

"Tell me, *Herr Kommandant*."

"I believe this: that Miss Nicola Fallaize was sent here for a purpose. It is impossible that she could hope to remain on the island unseen and undetected. Therefore, the English will have made a plan to take her off. There is only one way from Armorel, and that is by sea. The English will send a boat for her and that is the moment I wait for."

"But . . ."

"Listen to me, Müller. I have thought this out very carefully. The boat that the English will send will be a small boat. No big vessel could enter the shallow bays. But it is impossible that the English can know of the presence in Armorel of the gunboat *Lübeck*. They cannot know that the fastest gunboat in the German Navy is waiting for their arrival, with every gun manned. What I want, Müller, is not to sink the English vessel, but to capture it, its crew and its passengers intact. That is why the sentries on the cliffs have orders not to fire but to let the English come in. It is when they try to put to sea that we will have them."

"But, *Herr Kommandant*, do you think that an English boat will surrender? It is not the custom of the English Navy to surrender."

"If they do not surrender, they will be destroyed. I hope that they will not fight. It gives me no satisfaction to kill brave men." He frowned. "There is only one thing of which I am not certain. What is the purpose of Miss Nicola Fallaize? A thought occurred to me but it was so fantastic that I dismissed it. Now I am not so sure."

"May I know your thought, *Herr Kommandant*?"

"You may smile, Müller, but you do not know the English as I do. The French poet, Voltaire, called them 'engaging madmen' and he spoke after long observation. Here are the facts. Miss Nicola Fallaize, sister of the Suzerain of Armorel, is landed secretly on the island. The pedigree cow, Venus, property of her brother, vanishes and an attempt is made to substitute a painted creature. Mr. Lionel Fallaize, cousin and friend of this lady, is a painter. Neither he, the cow, nor Miss Fallaize are to be found." Weiss spread his hands. "Well, Müller, does any explanation occur to you?"

The Adjutant laughed.

"Surely, *Herr Kommandant*, you are not suggesting that the English sent Miss Fallaize to steal a cow."

"That is exactly what I am suggesting."

"But, but"—the Adjutant shook his head incredulously—"but as we sit here, our victorious Luftwaffe is burning London, the capital of England, to the ground. Everywhere in the world the English are being defeated. The war will be over in a matter of weeks, and Winston Churchill will be the prisoner of our Führer. *Herr Kommandant*, I repeat that at this moment London is in flames."

"Yes," said Captain Weiss drily, "and shall I tell you of an extract from one of our German Intelligence reports? The English have found it necessary to forbid the London firemen to enter burning buildings to save the lives of kittens."

"Kittens? Cows?"

"Yes, my friend. Kittens and cows." He stood up, threw away the end of his cigar, picked up the telephone and spoke rapidly in German to the gunboat Commander. The vessel was ready to put to sea at a moment's notice? The crews stood to their guns? Good. The Commander understood that only as a last resort should the English ship be sunk. The object was capture, not destruction. "I do not think that you will have long to wait, *Herr Kapitan.* I have a feeling that the time for action is nearly upon us. *Heil Hitler.*"

He put down the telephone, sat again in the armchair.

"All we can do now is to wait, Müller. Play me 'Frasquita' once again. I find this a very soothing song."

The Adjutant opened the piano once again. He played the melody once very softly. As his fingers moved towards the treble keys, the acid bit through the fuse and the first of Valentine Morland's time-bombs exploded with an ear-shattering roar in the desolate sands of Mermaid Bay.

The Adjutant's fingers whipped away from the piano. There was a second's quiet in which the rumble of the explosion echoed off the cliffs and caves of Armorel. Then Captain Weiss leapt to his feet. As he ran through the door he shouted, "Guard, guard. Turn out the guard."

Lionel Fallaize gazed on the extraordinary scene

before him. He saw it as a composition of darkness and of light, a composition which he knew with great sadness would never be transferred on to canvas for other eyes to see and to perceive. The flame of the candle threw a monstrous, sombre shadow across the shed. But the same yellow spear-point of flame found and glinted on Nicola's hair and glorified her head as she knelt, utterly absorbed in the task to her hands. He glanced at Sergeant Vogel—and was startled at what he saw. Though Vogel was ever watchful, though his finger was poised and ready in a split second to press the trigger of his Lueger, there was a look in his face of reluctant tenderness as he stood guard over a woman who tended a beast in labour. What strange alchemy had touched the heart of this hard and brutal man so that, in his proud moment of military triumph, he too heard the far-away pæan of the angels? And Alec Forbes, British Sergeant, captive of his enemy's bow and spear, how fared he in defeat? His face was eager, his eyes intent, his hands steady. He might as easily have been watching with joy the flight of a peregrine falcon in the wild, blown blue of a Hebridean sky. Valentine Morland stood as straight as a lance, his eyes looking at a thing which only he could see, his ears attuned to a song which only he could hear. Lionel's eyes moved on to Georges, their comrade in misfortune. The boy had hung his head and Lionel knew with a gush of sympathy the bitter thoughts of self-reproach that filled his mind. His heart went out to him in his distress and he dearly wanted to go to him and put his arm around those slender, shamed shoulders and say that it did not matter a damn and they were all brothers.

For a full minute the wind dropped and silence came over the woods. Then Sergeant Vogel spoke. His voice was gruff and not unkindly. "Now she can look after it herself. Go back against the wall, please."

Nicola brushed back her hair with her forearm. There was blood on her fingers. Crisis was over. The living calf had been delivered. Separate at last from its mother and the warm, blind darkness of the womb, the animate fruit of her long-forgotten mating sucked air into its lungs and blinked its bewildered eyes on the strange, cold and terrible world of men. Lionel said, speaking very gently:

"To Venus—a son."

Nicola glanced at him. She swayed on her knees. The calf lay on the ground, a wet bundle that breathed and made little sounds as tendrils of strength flowed into its free, unenclosed muscles. Venus had turned round and was licking it, eagerly, lovingly. Very slowly and deliberately, Nicola rose from her knees. One task was done. Now another, possibly the last of all, lay before her. She looked steadily at her cousin Lionel, trying with all the remnants of her strength to transmit an unspoken message to the man she knew and loved so well, and with whom she was one. He smiled at her. She believed that he understood. She turned her back on him and stooped down and gathered the new-born calf in her arms.

Sergeant Vogel backed. The brief moment of shared emotion had passed and he was once more an N.C.O. of the German Army with a gun in his hands. He was in command of himself and of the situation. He said:

"Put the calf on the ground. I order you to put the calf on the ground."

Nicola took a step towards him, her eyes dancing. He raised his Lueger and shouted at her, his mouth working:

"Put the calf down."

"But I want to show it to you, Sergeant Vogel. It's a bull-calf, the bull that my brother wanted Venus to bear. I knew—all the island of Armorel knew—that it would be a bull. Now Venus's son is in my arms, alive."

"Put the calf down and go to the wall. If you do not do so, I will shoot."

She came nearer to him, slowly and steadily. She was half-smiling and the calf's legs, jerking and kicking in their new-found strength, were a joy for her to feel against her body. She said softly:

"But you wouldn't shoot a little bull-calf, would you, Sergeant? You only shoot women and children, not calves. Not this one, anyway. This is the one they want in Berlin and—ah!"

The explosion of the timb-bomb in Mermaid Bay was like a thunder-clap. Sergeant Vogel jerked his head round to listen and in that second Lionel Fallaize sprang at him like a tiger.

Nicola's message had got through to her love and her twin.

CHAPTER TWENTY-ONE

TRANSIT OF VENUS

THE Provost of Armorel, gazing at the floor and turning his bowler hat over and over in his lumpy hands, heard the boom and echo of the time-bomb in Mermaid Bay. He took his massive silver watch from his waistcoat pocket and consulted it solemnly. Excellent. The first of the Major's infernal machines had exploded punctually. He heard a great stamping of boots and Captain Weiss's voice shouting orders. The Provost's escort, a fresh-faced youth from Bavaria who, for the last hour, had been puzzling over an old copy of *Signal*, jumped to his feet and grabbed his rifle. He ran to the door, stopped and looked back at the old man. He was confused and uncertain as to whether he should stay or go. The Commandant had shouted that the guard should turn out. He was one of the guard. Therefore he should join his comrades in the backyard of the Abbaye. But he had been told to watch the Provost, but what harm could this doddering old fool with the bowler hat do? *Ach ja. Natürlich!* A soldier always obeyed the *last* order he had been given. He came back into the room and said to the Provost:

"*Sie müssen hier bleiben. Verstehen sie?*"

"I do not understand German."

"*Gott verdammt!*" He struggled to find the right words. "You stay, you rest, here. It is forbidden to go. You understand?"

"Yes. Very good."

"I come again. You stay here."

"I hear you, monsieur." A volley of instructions from the Corporal of the Guard sounded from the yard. "Fall in. *Schnell, schnell.* All weapons to be loaded. Fall in on the left, you. Any man late on parade will be put in arrest. . . ." The Provost smiled. He said gently, "I think you had better go quickly, my friend."

The sentry undid the buckle of his cartridge pouch and ran to the door. When he had gone the Provost sat motionless for a brief space, listening to the shouting and the clatter in the yard. Then he put on his bowler hat carefully and walked to the half-open door. The hall was deserted. The Provost heard the measured ticking of the grandfather clock and, for a reason which he but half understood, he opened the walnut case and stopped the swinging pendulum. Then he went out by the hall door and walked into the windy darkness of Armorel.

"Lionel, are you all right?"

"Yes, I think so." He rubbed his bruised knuckles and winced. "I'm afraid that my instincts rather overcame my principles and, worse than that, I confess that I rather enjoyed it. I've owed Vogel that wallop for some time."

Valentine said drily:

"For a pacifist, you possess a quite remarkable upper cut. How's the patient, Alec?"

"I think his jaw's broken, Mr. Valentine." Alec turned Sergeant Vogel over and deftly knotted a cord round his wrists. Vogel opened his eyes and groaned. Alec said wistfully:

"You wouldn't shout, would you? Because if you did, this gentleman here would hit you one more clip and none of us would like that—much."

"We'll take him with us, Alec. The sea-trip will do his jaw good. Georges!"

"*Monsieur.*"

"There's a sentry on the *Pointe de Joie*. Do you think you can dodge him?"

"Me?" Georges was pathetic in his eagerness. "Of course I can. I know him. He's a nice man. His name is Johann."

"You have odd friends. Run like blazes to the *Pointe de Joie*. You'll find an M.T.B.—a British ship that is—lying off and a man with a big black beard. Tell him that we're coming, all of us. Alec, you've cut the telephone wire, haven't you?"

"I have."

"Good. Off you go, Georges. And if you do run into your friend the sentry, keep him talking. We're coming close behind you. Nicola, how soon will Venus be able to walk?"

"Now, if we take it easily. If I carry her calf, she'll follow."

"But isn't it heavy?"

She laughed with delight. She was full of joy.

"Heavy? Of course not. I love carrying it."

"Alec, you can look after Vogel. If he shouts or tries to make a break, shoot him—preferably in the stomach."

"I will. Venus ought to be milked out at once, but we can do that when we get her aboard."

Georges had already vanished into the darkness. Nicola took up the new-born calf in her arms. Prodded by the muzzle of Alec's revolver, Sergeant Vogel got to his feet and stood swaying. He mumbled, "Where do we go?"

"To England. We're going to introduce you to a kindly gentleman called Uncle George." He turned to Lionel. "What about you?"

Lionel said, smiling:

"Oh, I'll just come down and see you aboard. Now that I'm among friends, by the way, I'd like to confess to a past sin and get it off my soul."

"What is it?"

"It's only that I once won the Public Schools Middle-weight Boxing Championship." He gave a deep sigh. "That's better. Nicky, darling, are you all right?"

"I'm fine. Lionel, you can carry the mushrooms. They're a bit crushed, I'm afraid."

She walked to the swinging door, turned and showed Venus the calf in her arms. Venus followed eagerly, mooing softly after her son. With Alec Forbes's revolver in the small of his back, Sergeant Vogel stumbled to the door. Valentine and Lionel brought up the rear and the extraordinary cavalcade set out once more on its interrupted journey to England.

Georges wriggled through the bracken till he was well past the sentry post on the *Pointe de Joie* and then stood up and flew down the stony path to the strip of sand. He called out, "Monsieur . . . monsieur . . ."

Trawler Langley stepped forward from the darkness, his gun in his hand. He saw a small, panting boy.

"Oh, please, monsieur, have you a big, black beard?"

"I have. Have you got a cow?"

Georges peered at him. "Monsieur Trawler, it's you!"

"Of course it's me, Georges. Who did you think it was? The Emperor of Abyssinia? Where's Major Morland and Miss Nicola?"

"They are coming. All of them. They are coming now. Seven of them."

"Seven!"

"Yes. Seven. Five grown-ups and two children."

"Who the hell's coming?"

"When I say 'hell' my grandfather beats me. It is a bad word. Monsieur Valentine and Miss Nicola are coming, and their friend, Monsieur Alec. Also is coming Sergeant Vogel who does not want to come, and also Venus and her calf, who is now born and is a bull. And I am coming with you and Monsieur Lionel."

"But he's a bloody pacifist."

" 'Bloody' is also a bad word. It is worse than 'hell'. Monsieur Lionel is not a . . . what you said any more.

He hit Sergeant Vogel in the face. It was beautiful. He is coming with us. Please to wait for all of us."

"You'd need a battleship to carry that lot. Are there any Germans about?"

"Yes, Monsieur Trawler. There's one sentry on the cliff. Up there."

"Good. I'll just go up and . . . and talk to him while we're waiting."

"No, please don't do that. Don't talk to him. He's a nice man. His name is Johann and he gave me a cigarette to smoke last Friday. It made me sick. Please wait here. That is what Monsieur Valentine said. To wait here."

Trawler looked out to sea. Though the tide was already on the ebb, though the pulse of the water had become their mortal enemy, though every minute magnified the fearful risk he was about to take, he stroked his beard and grinned:

"All right, Georges. We wait. And if we miss this tide, we'll get the next. There's no hurry. No hurry at all."

Lionel Fallaize spoke softly in the wind-blown dark.

"Morland."

"Yes."

"You know the Provost's been arrested."

"Yes. I know. But they can't pin anything on him."

"Can't they! And you know that Baptiste was spotted when he tried to palm off the painted Hyacinth as Venus. So Baptiste is in trouble too." He smiled wryly. "Actually I was quite proud of my painting. I feel rather like someone whose *magnum opus* has been rejected by the Selection Committee of the Royal Academy. Captain Weiss is obviously a Philistine." He stopped smiling. "But quite a lot of people on this island will be in trouble—when you've gone."

"When *we've* gone?"

"Yes, when *you've* gone. I'm not coming with you, Morland."

The moon lifted a yellow tip over a dark streamer of cloud. Valentine glanced at Lionel. He was gazing straight ahead and his face looked as if it were carved in ivory.

Valentine said, "Tell me one thing. I only know you as 'Lionel'. What is your name?"

"My name is Fallaize."

"Ah."

"You see how it is."

"Yes. I see how it is."

The Corporal of the Guard came sweating up the path from Mermaid Bay and saluted Captain Weiss breathlessly.

"There is nothing, *Herr Kommandant*. Only explosive charges that make a big noise and do no damage."

Captain Weiss swung round as an orderly came running from the direction of the Abbaye. He gabbled the message that Captain Weiss half-expected.

"The sentry post at *Petit Pigeon* reports that a small vessel has rounded the headland and has made for the

Pointe de Joie. The telephone wire to the *Pointe* has been cut."

"It is as I thought. All troops will concentrate on the cliffs overlooking the *Pointe* at once. Men will take up their positions quietly and in no circumstances will a shot be fired until I personally give the order. I want a searchlight mounted on the cliff-head ready for instant use and all machine-guns are to be trained on the British vessel. Go quickly and quietly. I will follow when I've been to the harbour."

"*Zum Befehl, Herr Kommandant.*"

The end of the adventure was at hand. The raft with a well-padded horsebox on it dipped gently up and down on the sheltered tide as the breathless party came down the hill to the shore. Nicola, her arms aching, led the way, the struggling calf held against her breast. She saw Trawler and smiled at him wanly. He said:

"Give it to me, Miss Nicola."

"No. I can manage. I want to."

Very carefully she stepped on board the raft and turned and showed the calf to Venus, calling her with soft, affectionate, pleading words. Venus put one hoof on the floating platform, drew away. Nicola backed, came a step forward, backed again. Venus threw up her head. The calf gave a little frightened sound and kicked its spindly legs. Venus lumbered forward and entered the horsebox. Very gently, Nicola laid the calf on the straw and Venus bent over her son, licking him with her rasping, loving tongue. Nicola shut the door of the horsebox and leaned against it. Trawler said:

"All right, Miss Nicola?"

"All right, Trawler."

"Haul away. Take it easy."

The steel cable tightened and the raft was slowly drawn towards the M.T.B. It was at that moment that an extraordinary thing happened. Up on the cliff-head Captain Weiss gave a curt order and a brilliant white shaft of light sliced the darkness and shone on the tumultuous seas. The light moved over the water to the *Pointe de Joie*, steadied. In its beam Captain Weiss saw a fantastic sight.

The raft was alongside the vessel. Four steel pendants from the derrick were snapped into ringbolts on the four corners of the horsebox and the grotesque Botticelli was slowly airborne as the derrick lifted it evenly out of the sea and swung it towards the gaping hatch of the deck. Captain Weiss focused his field-glasses. He saw a girl scramble aboard . . . saw a bearded man with a little boy on his shoulders wade towards the vessel . . . saw a man in the uniform of a German Army Sergeant stumble into the water, driven by another man with a gun in his hand.

"*Herr Hauptmann*, permission to fire?"

"No. Wait. This is better than the Russian ballet. Our gunboat will be here at any minute and there is no escape for them. You saw who that was? Our good Sergeant Vogel."

Now another man was wading towards the vessel.

Captain Weiss saw him climb aboard and look upwards as the horsebox descended from the sky and disappeared into the hold. A faint roaring sound slid into the silence, a roar that seemed to come from the direction of the *Havre des Mouettes*. Captain Weiss chuckled:

"Here comes our gunboat."

The M.T.B. Commander shouted:

"All aboard?"

Valentine Morland answered from the stern:

"All aboard."

Nicola Fallaize looked swiftly round the deck.

"Where's Lionel?"

"He's not coming. All aboard, Skipper."

"But he is coming. I'm not going without him. I'm not. Lionel, wait for me . . . I'm coming ashore."

Captain Weiss heard the confused shouting. He saw the last batten being put on the hatch. He said sharply:

"Give one machine-gun burst astern of the vessel."

"*Jawohl, Herr Hauptmann.*"

The German machine-gunner peered along his sights, pressed the button of his gun. A jet of bullets rapped into the sea not three feet away from the vessel. Before the echoes of the firing had died away, Weiss heard a great shout from the bay below.

"Start up engines."

The Rolls-Merlin engines woke to life with all the strength of their four thousand horses. The two men and the boy had flung themselves flat on the deck and the girl was crouched by the stern, calling desperately to shore. Captain Weiss said quickly:

"One more burst."

A hose of bullets tore into the vessel's stern and splinters flew off the after deck.

"Slip forward."

As the cable splashed into the sea, there was an even louder roaring of engines and, to his delight, Captain Weiss saw the black bows of the German gunboat, creamed with parallel curves of foam, come swinging round the headland. He shouted triumphantly:

"*Gott seis gedankt.* We've got them. We've got them."

Trawler Langley looked round, saw his terrible enemy and grinned. He sprang to the wheel of the M.T.*B*.

"Full ahead together."

The M.T.B. shuddered and her wake streamed white behind her as she tore along the line of rocks. Trawler jerked his head round. The German gunboat was broad on his starboard quarter and she was overhauling him fast. In about thirty seconds she would be alongside—and he knew that he was heavily outgunned. Desperately he held the M.T.B. to her course, praying with all his strength. Suddenly, and with exultation, he heard a roar that came from the sky, a roar that even drowned the thunderous boom of his engines, as three Hurricanes in line ahead dived out of the racing clouds and swept the decks of the gunboat with cannon and bombs. Uncle George and the Royal Air Force had kept their appointment. Trawler Langley laughed. He shouted, "Stand by, everybody!" and swung the M.T.B.'s wheel hard a-port. The vessel heeled with a sickening lurch, swung back to an even keel. Like an arrow, Trawler Langley drove her straight for the suicidal channel of the *Couloir du Diable.* The wind took the shout from his mouth and flung his words over the sea. "Hold your hats on," yelled Trawler Langley, "we're going through!" and put her bows into the heart of the mountainous spray.

The wind and spume drove the breath from Nicola's body. She was drenched in the white smother of water . . . deafened by the crescendo of the engines . . . drowning in a choking swirl and then, suddenly, she drew a sobbing breath and looked up, wiping the spray from her eyes. She saw the White Ensign blowing stiffly at the yard and before her, the open sea. . . .

She was only conscious of a vast and enduring loneliness.

CHAPTER TWENTY-TWO

LA MAISON ÉTERNELLE

CAPTAIN HANS WEISS walked heavily up the path to Lionel Fallaize's cottage, kicked the door open. His face was lined and grey. He strode through the kitchen and into the studio. Lionel stood at his easel. He was painting with swift, confident strokes of his brush and he did not turn round. Captain Weiss stopped by the door, his feet astride. Lionel said: "Good morning, Weiss."

Captain Weiss made no reply. Lionel worked on in silence. It was a full minute before he stepped back and looked at his picture critically, his head on one side.

"I've been working on this for a long time. Now . . . now it's finished. It's called 'The Bridge'. I'm glad you didn't come until it was done." He turned round at last and faced Weiss. His face was white and strained but his eyes were bright. He put down his brush with an odd gesture of finality. "Now it's done."

Weiss said harshly:

"You know what has happened?"

"Not really. I know that they've got away, that's all."

"And do you know that the gunboat *Lübeck* has been sunk by bombing from the British Air Force?"

"No, I didn't know that. If any of the crew have been drowned, I'm sorry. I never wanted that."

"Seven German sailors and two officers have been picked out dead from the sea. Nine men are lying side by side on the shore, Mr. Fallaize."

"I'm sorry. I would like you to believe that I am sorry."

Captain Weiss looked round the studio with red-rimmed eyes. He saw the splashes of cow-dung on the floor. He said:

"So this is where Venus was hidden."

"Yes, this is where we took her, my cousin Nicola and I. Nobody else had anything to do with it, Weiss. Only Nicky and me. You must know that. Not the Provost, nor Baptiste, nor Jean, nor anyone on the island. It's true that Georges, the Provost's grandson, helped a bit and I can tell you that because he's gone with Nicky and the others. No one else knew anything about it."

"You wish me to believe that you alone are responsible?"

"On Armorel, I alone am responsible."

"What are you holding in your hand?"

"Some mushrooms. My cousin Nicky gave them to me. They . . . they were for breakfast in London."

Captain Weiss took a deep breath. He said:

"I have only one more thing to ask you, Mr. Fallaize. Why did you not go with your friends?"

Lionel walked to the window and looked out into the golden morning. The sun was up and radiant, the dew was on the grass and there was great excitement among the birds. Somewhere, far beyond the cliffs of Armorel, Nicky was at sea and safe and heading for home and Venus gave suck to her calf. No price was too great to pay for such glory. He said softly:

"How could I go? Someone had to be here to tell you the truth about what happened, or the whole island would be made to suffer. That's how things work out in this foulness called war. It is never the guilty who are made to endure, but the innocent. That's how things always work out when men forget God and peace and gentleness."

The two men gazed at each other. In stark and ugly clarity, Hans Weiss saw their two futures. He would be relieved of his post and court-martialled. His career as a German officer was finished and before him lay nothing but shame and humiliation for the creed of the new despots included neither understanding nor forgiveness. So much for Captain Hans Weiss, Panzer Grenadier, Commandant of Armorel.

But what of Mr. Fallaize? He saw the filthy formula that would inevitably follow: arrest, interrogation by the dehumanized ghouls of the Gestapo, loneliness, dirt, hunger and shameful death at the hands of a Nazi headsman. He would do much to save his friend from that, for this was a fine man and a man whose simplicity and sincerity shone like the morning sun. There could only be one way now—and might God forgive him for what he was about to do. . . . He said huskily:

"Keep looking out of the window, Mr. Fallaize."

The fear of death had often come to disturb his boyhood, but now Lionel was completely tranquil in the knowledge that death was close at hand. He saw the sweet curve of plough and the spread wings of gulls poised on the upper airs. Beyond the turn of the road, beyond the gates of the Abbaye of Armorel, the bell hung motionless in the tower where he and Nicky used to climb He braced his muscles and listened intently, waiting without fear for the moment when the bell would waken and swing and ring.

Its chime came suddenly and without pain. *Venez, montez à la Maison éternelle . . . venez, montez.*

LE MANOIR 1950–1951